Cutting it Short
The Bournemouth Writing
Prize 2022 Shortlist

Fresher Publishing
Bournemouth University

First published 2022 by Fresher Publishing
Weymouth House
Fern Barrow
Poole
Dorset BH12 5BB
www.fresherpublishing.co.uk
email publishing@bournemouth.ac.uk

Art Director: Saeed Rashid
Digital marketing and publishing assistants: Niamh Payne and
Kira Doak
Assistant editor: Milie Fiirgaard Rasmussen
Assistant Editorial Director: Belinda Stuebinger
Editorial Director: Dr Tom Masters
Cover design: Saeed Rashid/Niamh Payne

Foreword

Welcome to the 2022 Bournemouth Writing Prize shortlist anthology – a collection of the very best poems and stories the competition has to offer.

This is Fresher Publishing's debut shortlist anthology, with many more annual editions to come, and it is a testament to the incredible writing, originality, and inventiveness that the Bournemouth Writing Prize features every year.

The 2022 competition received so many extraordinary entries from across the globe, and we would like to thank every single person who entered, displaying lexical creativity, clever manipulation of form, and intriguing characterisation. In this anthology, witness the untold worries of old waxwork figures in Acrylic Eyes Yellowing Under Strip Lights in Acton, winner of the poetry category; join Jane and her troubling fixation in winning short story, The Prescription; and move with the haunting musicality of highly commended entry, The Man Who Loves Tchaikovsky Beats His Wife.

Many thanks are in order for our wonderful judges – with poet, Antony Dunn, in charge of the poetry division, and commissioning editor, Ansa Khan Khattak, and literary agent, Julia Silk, picking the winners of the short stories. We are also grateful to the MA Creative Writing and Publishing students for their commitment to the tough job of narrowing down hundreds of entries to create the longlist, and to Tom Masters and Bradford Gyori for producing the shortlist.

Thanks are also due to the staff working behind the scenes at Fresher Publishing. Firstly, to our editorial directors, Tom Masters and Belinda Stuebinger; to our assistant editor, Milie Fiirgaard Rasmussen; to our marketing and publishing assistants, Niamh Payne and Kira Doak; and to our art director, Saeed Rashid, for designing the cover.

Finally, a massive thank you to our former editorial director, Emma Scattergood, for her incredible work establishing Fresher Publishing and the Bournemouth Writing Prize, demonstrating a passion, devotion, and commitment that will live on here at the press. We wish her all the best for the future.

With everything said, we are proud to present you with all these wonderful poems and stories, and sincerely hope you'll enjoy *Cutting it Short*.

The Bournemouth Writing Prize Team
Fresher Publishing
Bournemouth University

Contents

Acrylic Eyes Yellowing Under Strip Lights in Acton

Ben Verinder

Winner

"Contrary to myth, Tussauds waxworks are never melted down to make new ones. They just go into storage." *Daily Mirror*, 21 October 2011

They came to mob whatever extract gave us power
scratch a nub of us beneath their fingernails,
frot us in the darker corridors then splurge
our currency down the Marylebone Road
but now we are stocked in rows.
Don't get blood on my shirt! Kennedy jokes
as Cobain fondles a cartridge between fingertips
smooth as soap. In winter, our hair rots
but this heat oozes us out of lousy clothes
as we watch Rutherford on her knees hunting eyebrows.
Gorbachev's port stain dribbles to his ear
and Victoria's fat head sinks into black bombazine
like the sun going down on Empire.
No visitor in weeks, only traffic rumbling
its imitation of the touch-up artist's trolley
and, from the workshop, a sewing hive,
voices, the gulp of boiling wax
poured into moulds. A revolution
is a struggle between futures and the past,
Castro replays. Voltaire is tongueless;

Ali, pinned by masonry bolts and webbing.
Frank won't leave the breeze of her open window.
Newman lost a hand. Even the Bonds are breaking.

The Prescription

Terry Kerins

Winner

It was as if a bag of wet sand had lodged on her chest, and with each breath, it got heavier and heavier, until it felt like her ribcage was no longer strong enough to keep lifting it up and down.

Dr. Griffin wrote her a prescription: antibiotics, steroids, an inhaler and the Xanax.

'The steroids can disrupt your sleep, let me give you something to help while you're on them. Xanax is a relaxant, it'll calm you down a bit as well until your breathing improves,' he'd said.

Sleep had been a problem long before the chest infection. It seemed that her life had become one big angry cry of 'Mammy!'. Sometimes, after a whole train of 'Mammies,' she'd snap 'round, 'What?' only to hear one of the children say, 'nothing,' and burst out laughing or crying, depending on the flavour of the day. That was, in contrast to Stephen. He said less and less. The spaces between his words stretched out and they were soon long enough to fit whole sentences. These created voids big enough for whole conversations to fall into. His body was still there, his mass an obstacle to get around in the house, but the longer the silences went on, the more he folded in on himself, his words and thoughts wound tight around him like a straitjacket.

Her chest got better, the antibiotics and steroids worked their magic, as did the Xanax. Shortly after taking one, it felt as if she was closing the door in a quiet dark room, shutting herself in to be able to shut down, to lose herself in sleep. It was such a respite. Once the steroid dose was finished, there was still a card and a half of the relaxants left. She put them in the zipper pocket of her handbag, ready to drop back to the pharmacy.

But the nights kept her awake. Stephen panned out in the bed beside her, tired after his day on the farm, an immovable boulder taking up more than his fair share of the space. The kids no longer needed her at night for feeds or cuddles. Sleep: it was what she'd longed for when they were smaller, but now it would not come. It would lower, start to settle, but then her heart would pinch, her whole body would jerk, leaving her wide awake again. The pale blue wisp of hovering sleep frightened away by her desperation and neediness.

The curtains in their bedroom were thin. They'd replaced his parents' blue and brown floral ones after the wedding. She'd chosen a maroon colour, remembering how exciting the decorating project had been. She hated the curtains now, any bit of light in the mornings turned the room into a raw pink cavity, like waking up inside of a mouth.

'Blackouts? What would we want those for?' he'd said when she'd suggested a change, 'sure we're in the middle of the fields, there's no one to be looking in on us.'

One night, a few weeks later, as Stephen lay on his back taking deep snorting breaths, she remembered the Xanax. Her bag was on the hook at the back of the bedroom door, and she took it to the bathroom. The bulb hummed and slime forming around the bar of soap by the sink caught her eye, a green upset against the white enamel. The zip-lock sleeve was still in the inside pocket of her handbag; thirteen tablets left. Biting one in half, she tucked the remaining half back into its foil cocoon. She washed it down with water from the tooth mug and went back to their room. For the first time in weeks, calmness spread, her body sunk below the level of the mattress, her brain formed a full stop and gorgeous sleep took over.

The next day, Jane was extra careful driving the kids to school, remembering the warning label: 'May cause drowsiness, take care when driving or operating machinery.' The last time she'd taken them, it had been at home to recover from the 'nearly pneumonia' as Dr. Griffin had called it. But up and about that day, the call of 'Mammy!' didn't seem as grating, nor did the broad wall of her husband's back as he washed his hands in the kitchen sink before dinner. She could block out the squelching his hands made as he lathered them, his muck merging with the mud from the potatoes in the colander, leading a greasy brown stream down the plughole.

That night, she took the other half – best not to return half tablets to the pharmacy. She'd swing by the next day and drop off the rest, a nice even dozen, or maybe even just wash them down the sink herself to save the trip. But somehow, neither happened and, almost as if by their own accord, the tablets dwindled, until one night there was only one half left. She popped it in her mouth, chewing it straight – it worked faster that way, its gritty bitter taste soon to be replaced by sweet indifference.

After dropping the children to school the next day, she made her way to the GP's surgery in the village.

'Hello, I'm wondering if I can make an appointment to see Dr. Griffin?'

'Oh, I'm afraid he's off this week. We have a locum, Dr. Rasheed, do you want to see him?'

Jane fiddled with the belt on her coat, 'yes, okay.'

'Just take a seat in his office, he'll be with you in a minute.'

Jane looked around the small room, remembering the last time she'd been there, struggling for breath. She remembered focusing on the poster of a pregnant woman cupping her bump, smiling in an ignorant-to-what-was-to-come way that only came with a first pregnancy. The poster was gone, replaced by a step-by-step guide to correct handwashing technique.

Dr. Rasheed was young and wore pointy shoes, 'Hello, Jane? I'm Dr. Rasheed,' he said with a perfectly formed Cork accent. 'How can I help you today?'

Jane held her breath for a moment before answering, 'it's for a repeat prescription.'

'Right,' the doctor frowned at the screen. 'Hmm... I don't see any regular medication.'

Her mind went back to a previous visit and the rash in the creases of her elbows that had brought her there, Dr. Griffin saying to just re-order the cream if needed.

'It's for the cream, and...' she added, 'the inhaler, you know, the blue one.'

'Right...'

'And, oh yes, the tablets that help with the breathing,' she said, gripping on to her hands to keep them steady. 'You see, I'd a bad chest, Dr. Griffin said they'd help when I'm feeling caught up.'

She took a raggedy breath as if to prove her point. Jane felt a blush filling up her cheeks and her eyes went to the poster again. *How, if Stephen spent so much time soaping and scrubbing, did his nails never seem fully clean, always with a furrow of earth under each one?*

The young doctor was focused on the PC.

'Okay, well, I don't see that on your file, but sometimes Dr. Griffin does handwritten notes,' he said, tapping the computer monitor as if it was somehow to blame. 'I'll give you a prescription for twelve tablets, but if you still feel short of breath or a bit panicky, please make a follow up appointment.'

'Thanks Doctor.'

A few weeks later, there was only one tablet left again. She took them whole now. Back in the consultation room, one corner of the handwashing poster was starting to curl up against the light green wall.

Dr. Griffin was back and quizzed her, 'would you say you are feeling joy in everyday life? Have you lost interest in your friends, your social life?'

What friends? What social life?

She pictured their sitting room when the kids were in bed: Stephen ploughing through a packet of chocolate digestives in front of the nine o'clock news, spraying crumbs as he shot curses at the meteorologist when he said the wrong thing.

'No, nothing like that, it's just the breath, I find the Xanax help with it.'

He made her blow through a cardboard tube, once, twice, three times, took her blood pressure and looked into the back of her eyes with a small torch.

He tapped away on the keyboard.

'Breathlessness is distressing, Jane. Try to get out, do a bit of exercise, maybe register for yoga in the community hall,' he said, before handing over the prescription at last. 'Some people find they get dependent on these; just watch how you go with them.'

She watched all right, as the little purple tablets counted down faster this time. 'A dental appointment' was her muffled line to Stephen the next time as she held on to her jaw. He frowned and handed over a fifty euro note, flicking it with his thumb and finger to make sure it was just one. Jane took it, hand unsteady, and went straight to the Corolla in the yard. The car indicated left for the village, but she continued past the shabby Colgate-smelling room that housed Dentist Carey and drove to the city.

The 24/7 walk-in GP clinic was on the quay. It was mostly made of glass and the watery sunlight reflected off it, bouncing spits of light off its corners, blinding Jane as she tried to read the bell number. The girl at reception had hostile, red nails filed to a point, and they clanked on the surface of the desk every time she moved her hands. She gave Jane a clipboard with a 'new patient' form to fill out and offered her a bottle of sparkling water. Jane fumbled with the clipboard, the pen, and the frigid water bottle. It rolled along the submarine grey carpet and came to a stop at a chrome table-leg. Jane sat and, once the form was filled in and the bottle safely parked on the table, she looked around the room. A single frame of what must be art, if money was no object, hung on the waiting room wall and there was no mention of handwashing. Everything looked so clean, correct handwashing technique was a given here.

Eighty euro later, Jane was back in the car in the multistorey carpark. The prescription was typed out, but at the bottom there was a hand-written 'repeat by one', followed by a squiggle and a sequence of numbers all joined together and slanting down the page. She found a black biro in the glove box and changed the 'one' into a 'nine' before folding the paper and tucking it in the zipper pocket of her purse. There was a late-night pharmacy beside Aldi, they'd fill it there for her on the way home.

Over Christmas, Stephen's brother and sisters and their families were all squeezed around the table, talking about the crops and the yield and the size of the turkey. The kitchen was too hot and too small for so many people, and it took one and a half tablets to get her to the same level of calm. She'd started off with just one, but somewhere between mass, with the reluctant children fidgeting beside her in the pew, and the endless requests for cups of tea or 'something stronger' afterwards, she'd bitten another half tablet off while in the downstairs loo. Carrying them around in her apron pocket was safest, especially with the younger kids in the house for the day.

The meal was late, it was nearly half past three before they sat down. She could feel her guests getting anxious, hovering and picking at the bowl of potato stuffing, her mother-in-law's recipe, 'especially for Stephen'. She'd been told it was his favourite that first year and now it was expected, even though Jane herself had always preferred a bread stuffing, loaded with onions, butter and herbs. Her in-laws all thought they had a right to sit and be waited upon, just because they'd sat at the same table every day as children and eaten breakfast there. Stephen sat in his father's seat and, when he did the honours and carved the bird, his brother and sisters clapped. The children joined in, Jane's hands were full with the bowl of roast potatoes.

Once the plates were loaded, she drank the festive glass of red quickly. The mound of brown and beige food on the plate in front of her looked unappealing. A gravy coated brussels sprout lay abandoned on the tablecloth. *Later on, it'll be murder to get the stain out.* The wine on top of the Xanax made her able to sit through the meal slightly removed from the racket and the clatter. She felt held in a heavy velvet hammock. The talk and emotions bounced off her and doubled back to strike those around her at the table in an invisible tennis rally.

After dinner, while alone doing the washing-up, she poured more of the wine into a reindeer mug belonging to one of the kids and drank it in one go. Rinsing the mug, she watched the reindeers circling around it, galloping, galloping, galloping on a pointless treadmill. The mug would soon be put away until next year, only to be taken out again so they could continue on their dead-end merry-go-round. She wondered if the mug would retain the taste of the wine and whether the next hot chocolate would sense its unfaithfulness.

'Silly notions,' she said under her breath and turned off the kitchen light behind her.

The rest of the adults were glued to *Mrs. Brown's Boy's*

in the sitting-room. The children were in the den, worn out from the early start and the added chaos the cousins brought. She looked at Stephen and saw him as he was before. Before his father's death and his mother's insistence that he 'defer for a year'. Before the boundary issue and the trouble with the neighbours, before the two blue lines and the hurried wedding, before the coldness crept in. She saw him at the Debs, tanned from a season of football, in his rented tuxedo, ready to go to Dublin. Now his check shirt strained to close, his middle spilling over the belt of his trousers, and there was a hole in the toe of one of his socks. He caught her looking at it and slid his foot over the carpet so the flabby sock rolled the hole under his foot.

'Anyone for a top-up?' He asked, looking straight at her and, for one minute, it seemed like Stephen could see through it all as well. But dullness settled behind his eyes, his mouth sealed closed. He went around the room with the bottle, filling his brother and sisters' glasses, their spouses', his own and, by the time he came to her, there was none left. He stood in front of her with the empty bottle in his hand. He held it out and put it in hers before turning and sitting back down in the chair nearest the fire.

Jane's eyes smarted, his own glass was full well past the little white line on it that measured 'a unit'. He'd come back from the Co-op one day with a box of six. She'd been delighted, her mind jumping to something luxurious, a rare present, only to discover a set of half a dozen 'Drink Safely' wine glasses: 'On sale, going for half nothing'. They used them when visitors came over, which wasn't often, and she turned the white line to the opposite side, hoping no one would notice it.

Jane got up, went to the cold back kitchen and put the empty bottle in the recycling. She stood at the narrow, single paned window by the back door and looked into the

Christmas night; into the stillness. At the end of the yard stood the hayshed, a hulk of a structure, the light on its gable end cast a dirty orange glow in the muddy paddock. *Far from a Christmas welcome*, she thought as she strained her eyes to see past it, to look deeper into the night. But beyond was just blackness.

She took a step back from the window and it filled up with the reflection of her own face, distorted like a stroke victim against the muzz of drizzle at the other side of the glass. Her hand found the sheet of Xanax and her fingers released one into her palm. She saw it in the jarring light of the bare bulb, saw her choices, saw her no choices. She could put it back, grind the remainder of the tablets in the garlic press and be done with them. Honour her vows, show up at community centre for yoga. But instead, she put it on her tongue and chewed until it was just an unpleasant aftertaste swallowed in a dry gulp.

She turned and faced the sitting-room, the door was ajar as the fire was too hot for the mild evening. Stephen had built it up too far and it licked the sides of the hearth with its greedy tongues, swallowing all the freshness in the room. Her husband's head turned, seeing her in the hall, waiting for her to go back to take her place. It would soon be time for tea and turkey sandwiches. She'd have to cut the Christmas cake, and the tin of sweets would be passed around again.

Dainty

Faith McNamara

I've always wanted to be smaller
To take up less space
Fall below prying eyes
No longer be right there, in your face

My limbs to be wiry thin
Like that in a flower found
Constantly wrestled by the winds
But always rooted to the ground

Oh, to be seen as a fragile bird
Something to be clutched at and held
Clasped in strong, weathered hands
Hand fed ideas to believe in and beheld

But I am not these things
I am large and loud
Screaming out my thoughts
Always standing out in a crowd

Though I've always wanted to be smaller
Maybe it's okay to occupy this space

Molding

Milie Fiirgaard Rasmussen

Shall I compare us to a sourdough?
So rare and tepid, kneading your embrace.
We stir and bend as bodies fit a mold,
while heat do rise 'round shivers to erase.
A push past lines, entwined; yet not all spoken
with syrup voice, call quaint lit streets a home.
With acts of scoring; flesh calmly opened.
Short breathing revealing the shells' shy moan.
Our walls of steal seal stress and mess away.
This pot lid that did fit nicely, until
it touched the crust. We clean another day.
Ferment; content with spots, we see them still
      as heat so sweet can carry voices clear:
      To grow and learn, I burn and stand still here.

The Rescue Dog
David Butler

13a Drummond Close had an abandoned air, as though some daemon of neglect had breathed over it and moved on. Even in the early April sun, the house remained colder than its neighbours. Sicklier. The brickwork had a lichen-green pallor that extended over the windowpanes. So, too, over the Nissan that had been decaying on its driveway for two years now.

'Hello?' she called.

She had to jimmy the key in the lock, turn it through a number of revolutions before the mechanism gripped and the door juddered open.

'Anybody home?'

The air was hangover stale, sharpened with an acridity that made Muireann think of solitary maleness. A tang that recalled visits to the zoo. Not for the first time, there was a hint of a more disturbing odour, a corrupt stench you'd maybe catch off old cardboard laid under bridges. She hesitated to pull the hall-door shut behind her.

'Anybody in?'

In answer, the cascade of a toilet erupted to the far end of the corridor.

'Hoi, d'you never think to crack open a window in here?' she called, veering into the kitchen and jerking aside the net curtain, though the liver-spotted window refused to budge.

He appeared in the doorway behind her, an unshaven, broad-shouldered man with the beginnings of a belly. He had on a vest and tracksuit pants, and his hair was wet as though he'd just dunked it in a basin.

'That's some collection of bottles you have in your recycle bin, Frank.'

He took a while before answering, as though he wasn't sure

what tone to select.

'Rough night last night.'

'Ha! I almost believe you.' She'd tugged open the back door, a draft of cooler air entering with the daylight. 'Seriously, how many are you putting away these days? And don't give me Grandad's oul guff about wine being a great man for the cholesterol.'

'The trick is to avoid opening the second bottle.'

'Yeah?'

He'd hoisted up his features, a mask to suggest levity.

'I account it a small victory not to have the first tipple before the six o'clock angelus.'

'Seriously. How many a week?'

'What is this, an inquisition? Did my loving sister send you over to spy on me?'

'As if!' She looked hard at him. 'You'll do yourself serious damage. Multiple organ failure, yeah? It's no joke, Frank.' Because that was the odour she'd caught, unmistakable now he'd exited the bathroom. 'Look how Grandad wound up.'

'I daresay the old man had his demons to fight.'

'I've always hated that expression. It glamourizes the whole thing. Like being a dipso is meant to be heroic or something.'

'A *dipso*? Jesus, I haven't heard that expression in donkeys.'

Now she was rooting in the fridge. Checking its alcohol content, he had no doubt. She lifted out a packet of mince more brown than red, made a show of inspecting the 'Reduced to Clear' label.

'Really?' she inquired. 'Is it any wonder Aunty Joyce left you?'

'That's unkind. Also inaccurate. I'd never dare buy 'Reduced to Clear' back in Joyce's day.'

'You did so! She told me. She said you'd ease off the labels. She always knew because the bar-code would be faded and torn.'

'That is a lie!' he declaimed theatrically.

She shut the fridge. 'You do remember what's happening today?'

'Today?' He stretched one arm up against the lintel, rubbed lazily at an armpit. 'Sure, maybe you'll remind me.'

'Go on with you now, you know well what today is.'

He watched her avoid seeing the calamity of pots and plates in the sink. Detaching himself from the doorframe, he made a pantomime of searching around the room, behind the armchair, under a cushion, beneath the table upon whose faded oilcloth lay a screwdriver, a radio and the entrails of a plug.

'Where is it, so? Jaysus, it must be one of those whatcha-may-call-em, bug-eyed, shivery little rats looks the spit of Peter Lorre...'

'Beena's bringing him along later. I said I'd throw an eye over the place, make sure there's nothing he might choke on. He's called Blue, by the way.'

'So what make of dog is he, anyhow?' He'd lifted the screwdriver and plug, put on unlikely glasses. 'Can I've three guesses?'

She shrugged, prepared to be amused.

'How big did you say?'

'Small. Size of, I dunno... a pillow?'

'A *pillow*.'

She'd begun to potter across the linoleum floor with dustpan and brush.

'Or... a grab-bag.'

'My God, your comparisons! And you an English teacher.' He laid down the items, frowned, tucked one hand under either armpit. 'He's one of those Presbyterian tykes with the Old Testament eyebrows, what's this they're called?'

'A schnauzer?' She hoisted her eyebrows dismissively, a real teacher's trick that. 'I'll help you out. Blue's not any type of terrier.'

'Not a terrier. Oh Jesus. A poodle.'

'You're such a fecking…' She clattered the dustpan into a corner. 'No.'

'Not a poodle.' He raised his arms in token surrender. 'You got me, kid. Go on, what?'

'We don't know for sure. Bulldog cross?'

'Bulldog. Cross meaning vicious, is it?'

'Yeah right! He's four months old, like.'

'Neutered?'

'Intact.'

'House-trained?'

' -ish.' She hovered a hand equivocally. 'You might keep an odd newspaper handy.'

'A bed-wetter, and muscle-bound as a bouncer, I'll be bound. And with a puss on him like one of them bunched up, soft-leather grab-bags your Hindi pal is so fond of.'

Muireann stood rigid, allowed the humour to evaporate.

'She has a name you know.'

He found again the screwdriver, busied himself with the plug.

'I daresay she does.'

'Beena.'

'Well, it's Beena pleasure…'

'Ha, ha!' Avoiding the clutter, she filled the kettle from a stuttering tap. 'What do you have against her? I've never known.'

'Against her?' He peered above his bifocals, waited. She noticed the tremble in his fingers was back.

'I have nothing against her,' he said. 'She scares me, is all.'

'She scares you.'

'It's the hair. *Those dreads, man.* The way she wears them half bunched up, as if some giant tarantula had nested on her head. You know how I am with spiders.'

She busied herself with detergent and bucket while the kettle rattled voluminously to the boil.

'I suppose only West Indians are allowed to have dreads, yeah?'

'Hey, you're the generation is meant to be "woke", Muireann ní Bhriain. I'm a relic from the Dark Ages, remember?'

'I never said that.' She'd begun to shove the mop in energetic swipes over the surface.

'Sure you did. Christmas?'

'You weren't there at Christmas.'

'Your birthday, then.'

'You haven't been anywhere next or near Mam's in well over a year. Not since Joyce…'

'Yeah. Least said. My, doesn't time fly?' The mutinously shaking fingers abandoned the task of wiring. 'What's the deal, remind me. A week's babysitting, was it?'

'Ten days. Two weekends, remember? We arrive back on the twentieth.'

'Hitler's birthday.'

'And someone else's. The half century, isn't it, Frank?'

'Don't remind me. Eyesight getting longer, temper getting shorter.'

'Mam can't take him on account of the cats.'

'Peculiar time to adopt a dog just when you guys knew you were going away, or no?'

She leaned on the mop. 'You're not going to back out on me, Frank?'

'No, no. *Morituri te salutant.*'

A first exchange of smirks was interrupted by a peremptory thump at the front door.

'That'll be Beena now.'

A cascade followed, as if a hundred tiny ball-bearings had spilled and scattered. The bulldog pup that scampered into the kitchen was everything he'd imagined. Tubular. Muscular.

An asthmatic, scrunched up muzzle flanked by Churchillian jowls. Its coat was so soft it might've been made of suede and be-damned if it didn't have a blue hue to it.

What disconcerted were the human eyes. An old man's eyes.

While Beena – dungarees, nose-stud – hefted two shopping bags and a dog-harness onto the counter, unsettling the sink's clutter, Frank scooped the pup up onto the table.

'Give the floor a chance to dry off,' he said vaguely.

The pup took a single sideswipe from a bowl of water Muireann set beside it, then stood rigid as a statue, its old man's eyes never for a second leaving Frank's. He, equally aware of Beena's ironic scrutiny, hunkered down.

'You are one ugly motherfucker, you know that?' he cooed, scratching behind the undersized ears.

A moment later, a response rose from the table's oilcloth. It took the form of a snare-drum rattle that sent flippant blobs of amber wobbling like mercury across the plastic, dribbling over the precipice and piddling to the floor.

'That's telling you, Frank,' said Beena.

Once they'd left, any frivolity caved in. He'd watched from the gate Muireann's hatchback diminish until it was swallowed by the T-junction. At once, the afternoon yawned open. The aching, interrogative silence of it. And the one after, and the one after that, and the whole stretch of featureless time till his niece returned, the ten last dismal days of his forties. When he held it flat above the gate, his hand was trembling like an aspen leaf. Old anxiety began to fill his gut with static. The fear. The giddiness. Had he been able, he'd have run after the car, called out after her,

'I can't, Muireann! I can't fucking manage.'

Returning into the interior, damp now with detergent, it was almost a surprise to find the dog hadn't moved. It stood erect on the kitchen table, the plugless radio mute beside it.

'You really are one ugly mother,' Frank repeated, to make a breach in the silence.

He extracted from one of the shopping bags a twin-pack of kitchen-roll, bandaged a few sheets about his hand. He then wiped down the oilcloth, making no allowance for the pup whose knowing eyes followed the movements even as the paws were made to prance.

He pulled off the makeshift glove, dropped it to the floor and moved it with his foot over the yellow splashes. He then pincered it up, marched to the bathroom, flicked it into the toilet and, after working the handle like a defective pump, finally discharged it.

Back in the kitchen, he considered what to do next. The wash-up he'd save for later. The mincemeat and rice would keep, too.

'Ok,' he sighed. 'Ok.'

In one movement, he opened a press, lifted a wine bottle, weighed it with a toss, needlessly checked the label – they'd been identical since the Lidl sale last January – set it upright on the counter and twisted the cap. He'd lied to his niece. It wasn't the six o'clock angelus he accounted a small victory, it was the twelve o'clock. Today, he'd beaten it by forty-five minutes.

He'd also lied when he'd said the trick was to avoid opening a second bottle. It was the third bottle that was the problem. But that was a problem for later.

He poured a mug, the white enamel blackening the wine. But he didn't down it at once. Instead, from the other shopping bag, he drew out an open bag of kibbles.

'A quarter cup in the morning, a half in the evening. Wasn't that it, buddy?'

The eyes watched him.

'Sure, a handful never hurt anyone, huh?'

He rattled a few in a breakfast bowl, set it down in front of the bulldog. Toad-like, it passed a tongue twice over its nose, but it didn't so much as sniff the offering. Frank raised the mug, toasted the visitor and tossed off half the contents.

'Suit yourself,' he wheezed as the burn travelled down the raw gullet and into his gut.

Steadily worse each day, as though his innards were being corroded. He really should make a determined effort to get some soakage in in advance. But the last time he'd checked the breadbin, the sliced pan was freckled with verdigris.

Of one thing Muireann was right: he was slowly killing himself. Of that, there could no longer be any doubt. Some mornings, he'd caught the same fetid waft from his urine that he knew from his old man's decline. But here was the thing: he'd been on such a continuous binge now – months on end it had lasted – that any short hiatus risked paranoia; the afternoon jitters, the unfathomable sorrow that came from nowhere, heavy as swamp water. The anti-depressants were no bloody use against that. It gave him the jitters just to think about it.

At least he avoided spirits, most nights.

He was slowly killing his bank account, too. At this rate, he'd be out of the house by the next birthday following. After Joyce had left, he'd considered taking a lodger into the back room to stem the haemorrhage. What stopped him wasn't so much the thought of sharing the bathroom and kitchen. Not even TV rights. The company itself mightn't have been such a bad thing. What he'd balked at was the idea of having a stranger's scrutiny turned on him, seeing how every day was the same as the next, every night, Friday and Saturday, spent on the sofa. Fuck that.

He'd fallen out of the habit of talking. Aside from niece and sister, there was no-one. How had he let that happen? How had he allowed the slow disintegration of a marriage swallow up all his energy? Dole office once a month, post office every Wednesday, twice a week to the supermarket. These were the only features on the map of his solitude.

It was a small mercy Muireann had always liked him; looked in on him once in a way. Less often, now she'd hooked up with your one with the dreads and dungarees. At the sound of her car on the drive, he'd hoist his old, jaunty humour like a tattered flag, let on he was doing ok. And for the couple of hours she'd sit in with him, maybe he was.

Reaching for the bottle, his hand brushed off something unexpected. The harness clattered to the floor. It took him a moment to recognise it.

'Come on,' he called, gruffly. 'We'll go out for a breath of air.'

April twentieth was a day of relentless drizzle. At least it meant they were home when Muireann finally called. For some reason, he'd expected her in the morning.

Beena was with her. She brooded at the threshold of the kitchen as though fearing contagion, which was ironic; Frank had made a real effort to tidy the house. Blue, meanwhile, was bouncing on hind-legs and hugging Muireann's calf tight as any marsupial, the tail-stump rapid as a wiper up full.

'How's my fella, huh? How's my little maneen?' she fussed, in that baby-talk that all the women seemed to adopt in the pup's presence.

'Three DVDs he demolished. One slipper. I'll send the bill. I'll tell you another thing,' Frank went on, 'he's a bit of a scrapper, so he is. So that first day I took him on up to Corkagh Park, this one with a red setter and a big hairdo comes over. Orthodontic grin. American, of course.

"Look at you! Aren't you *cute*?" Cute!? "What is he," she goes, "Staffy?" I said he could be a bloody Pitbull for all I knew, all I could say with any certainty was he's a rescue dog, and aren't the most of them fellas mongrels? Our pal there is standing stock still, not at all sure what to make of the attentions the setter is giving him. Sniffing here. Pawing there. But Muireann, you want to have seen the look of comical concern when the setter finally decides to stand astride him.

"Aren't you just a-*door*-able?" Well, adorable or not, the next thing he's launched himself at the setter's throat like a Tasmanian Devil, you'd swear it was a rabbit he was going for and not a mutt five times his size. Our American friend is outraged, says how I shouldn't be let in the park if I can't control my dog. I had to laugh though. That anxious look he gave, as much as to say, *what the hell are you up to?'*

'They're a great way to meet people,' Muireann glanced up from her struggle with Blue's uncontainable excitement. 'It's like there's this whole community of dog owners out there. Only, it's the dog that owns the owner, not the other way 'round.'

'All I can tell you, he's not afraid to take on anything. The size of the fight in the dog, isn't that what they say? You'll have your hands full with him.'

'And c'mere, where did he sleep?'

'Sleep?'

'Yeah.'

He glanced toward Beena, who was watching complacently from the doorway. Was it a trick-question?

'You never left over any bedding.'

'I know that. What I'm asking, where did he sleep?'

Be-damned if there wasn't some sort of a look fired between the two girls. Some sort of codology.

'Sure, how would I know where he slept?' He looked about. 'On the sofa, I suppose.'

'He did, aye.'

'I don't know what you're trying to imply.'

She pushed the dog away, its paws sliding stubbornly across the linoleum.

'I'd say you'd miss him all the same, Frank.'

'Wait a minute. What do you mean I *would* miss him?'

'Happy birthday, Uncle!'

'Ah, no. Oh no you don't…'

'What?'

'You're not foisting your mongrel on me, girl.'

Beena detached herself from the doorway. 'You'd want to be careful, Frank. Owners come to look like their pets, isn't that what they say?'

'No way. No way, José.' He glared at his niece. 'I knew well you were up to something.'

'Tell you what,' she said, wiping the cobweb of slobber from her trouser-leg. 'Hold onto him for another month. Yeah? See how you get on. If you don't want him at the end of that, I'll get in touch with the shelter. Deal?'

He looked at the mutt, whose imperturbable gaze was now directly on him.

'A month?' he said.

Today

Viktoria Filipova

I'm sorry sun –
I missed today,
I missed your love,

                I missed your touch.
                I saw the moon,

                                I told her you
                                were gone today,
                                I missed you much.

I'm sorry sun –
I got away,
I wasn't there

                for you to preach,
                and I'm a liar –

                                I won't reach
                                the sky, in which
                                you turn.

I'm sorry sun –
I missed today,
I'll miss tomorrow

                out of love,
                I saw the moon –

                                I said, good day,
                                so she won't know
                                that you were gone.

And oh, your sunset
went unwitnessed –
the sky outburst

                    a shade of sorrow,
                    and those who love,

                                      and who will miss
                                      it,
                                      will not know
                                      until tomorrow
how much
today
is

                    missing

                                  us.

Taxidermy

Anna Seidel

A silver crystal owl scent bottle burst
on her day of death, unearthing the ground.
Bearing a bounty of hidden treasures,
each subtly enveloping a story
of life's ephemeral nature.

The scent of leather flower settles
in a near century-old bowl,
still marked by the shining drool
of rattling stray dog teeth, she'd fed,
while listening for a rhythm,
in their abandoned souls' screaming.

Perfume spills on the typewriter she used,
to build, bit by bit, the advance obituaries
of dotty dictators with.
Duck decoys on her desk still hold notes
pulled from her marvelous, magpie mind,
cluttered with all sorts of useless information.

She knew
the color in a pitch-black room was "eigengrau".
She knew
cats couldn't taste sweets due to genetic defect.
She knew
apple seeds contained cyanide.

Folded over the back of her chair still
"The Art of French Cooking" rests,
opened on "Tarte Tatin",

holding the secret of at least four lovers
encrypted in penciled ingredient lists.
Memories continued in silence,
sawdust fillers to curious dioramas
that kept those we love alive.

Father's Day

Chris Cottom

Highly Commended

I was ten minutes early, but Dad was waiting on the bench in his tiny front garden.

'I've been enjoying the sunshine,' he said, as if I'd never twigged that his true joy was punctuality.

After brushing a non-existent speck from his cavalry twills, he pushed down on his walking-stick to get to his feet. He squared his shoulders as best he could, trying to conjure the six-footer he'd once been. His saggy cheeks were freshly shaved, he smelt carbolic-clean, and his crinkly white hair shone with the bay rum with which he'd dressed it daily for at least the last fifty years.

'Happy Father's Day,' I said, holding out the present I'd got him. As he tucked it under his arm, I thought maybe he wanted to shake hands.

'Thanks Tim.'

'Not asking me in? I need a wee.'

He unlocked the door, and I ran up the stairs to the pink bathroom, poking my head into the galley kitchen afterwards. As I expected, the draining-board was empty; he'd have washed and dried his breakfast things, having eschewed the dishwasher since Mum died, claiming it took him a week to fill it. The place had the reassuring tang of disinfectant. The cleaners were doing a good job.

'Nice new motor,' Dad said, unbuttoning his blue blazer before pulling his seatbelt across, careful to avoid his breast pocket with its red silk handkerchief crisply folded into three ascending peaks. 'What do you get to the gallon?'

'Haven't a clue. You're not going to make me calculate cost per trip, are you?'

'Didn't do you any harm, did it? A spot of mental arithmetic, now and again.'

No holiday had been complete without it.

'It's harder now the pumps are in litres,' I said. I didn't tell him my employers paid all my petrol anyway. Just as I hadn't wanted to embarrass him years ago when I'd realised, aged twenty-eight, that my salary was higher than his had ever been.

My present was on his lap. 'Aren't you going to open it?'

'I guess it's a CD.'

He'd always been a classical man, sharing with Mum a lifelong love of choral works.

'That's right,' I said, 'Deep Purple's Greatest Hits.'

His smile told me he'd accepted the joke, as I'd known he would. He slipped his gnarly thumb under the edge of the wrapping paper.

'*The Complete English Anthems*. The Tallis Scholars. Delightful. Can you put it on?'

'Sorry, they don't put CD players in cars nowadays.'

'Cheap Japanese rubbish,' he said with a laugh.

'I'll see if I can find the Tallis on my phone.'

'Not while you're driving, please.'

'How've you been, anyway?'

'Fine. Absolutely fine. Perhaps we could have some music, though.'

I stopped, searched my phone and found Bach's *St Matthew Passion*. Before I let him listen to it, I wanted to know what the consultant had said about how he was doing.

'Dad, tell me–'

'Are we going or not?' he said, checking his wristwatch.

I said nothing, pressed 'play' and turned the volume up. I wanted this to be a happy day out. We were off to have a look round his old college.

We did the Park & Ride from Headington into Oxford. Dad's eyes were everywhere, particularly when we crossed Magdalen Bridge into what he called the 'city proper'. We got out at the Examination Schools and walked back to Merton Street. The Eastgate Hotel on the corner, Dad told me, was where he'd got a taste for Watney's bottled brown ale. He pointed out Number 21, where he assured me Tolkien had lived, and, on the corner, the incongruously modernist house of the Warden.

'He and his wife would have all the freshmen to dinner in batches,' he said. 'She had a buzzer on the underside of the table to summon the minion from the kitchen to clear the plates. They liked taking their holidays in the South of France. There was some rumour this meant nudist camps.'

As the occasional car rumbled over the cobbles, we ambled along the pavement beneath the high flinty wall, over which, Dad said, generations of stop-out Mertonians had been forced to clamber.

'Eventually, the university gave up curfews as a bad job. Got rid of the bulldogs.'

'Bulldogs?'

'Their private police force. Wore bowler hats. You were in big trouble if they caught you. Before my time. We all had keys to the late gate here.'

We strolled past the entrance to the college and stepped across the road to stare up at the chapel, its huge square tower dominating the little street.

'I went up there with your mother once,' Dad said, softly and without looking at me. 'On May Day, about five o'clock in the morning, a group of us from the choral society. None of us had gone to bed the night before. The ladies all wore summer dresses, with flowers in their hair. As the sun rose, we sang madrigals to welcome the first day of spring. Afterwards, we

43

took a punt out and had breakfast on the Cherwell, just me and your mum; she'd made a picnic. It was still misty before it warmed up.'

In the entranceway to Merton, a painted wooden board proclaimed that the college grounds would open to visitors at two-thirty. We'd made good time on the M40; it wasn't even one o'clock.

'You're not a visitor, you're an alumni,' I told Dad.

'Alumnus, actually. Alumni's the plural. There's only one of me.'

'Alumnus, old Mert, whatever.'

I stepped around the sign and into the porters' lodge. Three walls were covered with pigeonholes, bulging with flyers, envelopes and small packets. At a small counter behind the glassed-in fourth wall sat a man in late middle-age wearing a jacket and tie. He looked up from his *Daily Express* and slid his wooden-framed window aside.

'Can I help you sir?'

I explained that my father was an old Mertonian, and we'd like to look around.

'I'm afraid you'll have to come back after two-thirty, sir.'

'Even though he's a member of the college?'

'Even though he's a former member of the college, yes sir.'

'One other thing. Dad told me that, as an undergraduate, he could go up the chapel tower. I know how much he'd love to go up one last time, before... before it's too hard for him.'

'I'm sorry sir, members of the public are no longer permitted access to the tower. Health and safety, you see.'

I sensed that Dad had stepped into the lodge behind me. I leaned in a little closer and kept my voice low.

'He's seventy-nine and not... I mean, I don't think we'll be able to make another trip. If there's any way...'

I wanted to say I'd make a donation to a rebuilding fund of their choice, or endow a bookcase of first editions, or slip this jobsworth a fifty.

Instead, I said, 'It's Father's Day.'

The porter looked past me at Dad, who was standing a few steps back, spruce in his summer-weight blazer, crisp white shirt and Merton tie.

'Well… come back at two-thirty. No promises, but I'll see what we can do.' He even smiled as he slid his window shut.

Dad followed as I negotiated our way out through a gaggle of elderly tourists. On the pavement, an Asian couple wore matching raincoats, securely belted against the sunshine.

'What were you talking about?' Dad said.

'Nothing. Just asking him where we might get some lunch.'

Dad had equipped himself with his stout brown brogues, re-soled over decades and polished to parade-ground perfection. But we still made slow progress on the short walk past Corpus Christi and Oriel to The Bear, a rabbit warren of a pub boasting similar antiquity to Merton itself. Its walls and even its ceilings were eccentrically bedecked with snippets of men's ties, closely packed in huge glass display panels, each exhibit meticulously labelled in sometimes faded handwriting.

Dad laboured over his pint and his ploughman's, his arthritic fingers struggling to balance cheddar and pickle onto his baguette, which then proved a challenge for his dentures.

'They'll have a Merton tie here,' he said, dropping crumbs on his own.

'I'm sure they will.'

'Merton and this place have been neighbours forever. I should think it kicked off the collection.'

'Don't ask them to show you,' I said. 'It'll take them until Armageddon to find it.'

He pushed his plate away, half his lunch untouched.

'I'm not terribly hungry,' he said, wiping his mouth.

'Dad, tell me. What did the consultant say?'

'I told you. I'm doing fine.'

'Really?'

He looked at his watch and reached for his stick.

'Didn't that sign say the college opened at two-thirty?'

Dad clicked his tongue when we got back to Merton at two-fifteen to find tourists already queuing. As we shuffled to the back of the line, the porter stepped out onto the pavement.

'There's the young man you were talking to,' Dad said.

'You need your eyes tested. That chap isn't young, not in anybody's book.'

'Of course he is. Can't be much more than sixty.'

The porter beckoned us and took us into his glass-screened Holy of Holies. He sat my father down at his little desk and explained that, if we would both kindly sign a disclaimer, he would let us have the key to the chapel tower.

'Would you like me to take you over there?' he said.

'I know the way, thanks,' my father said. 'Through Mob Quad. It's only sixty-one years since I matriculated.'

'Two things, sir. Do take care, some of the steps are quite steep, as I'm sure you'll remember. And the lights are automatic now, they're movement sensitive. Oh, and Happy Father's Day, sir. May I ask what you were reading when you were up?'

'Biological Sciences,' Dad said. 'All completely out of date and useless now.' He laughed. 'Like me.'

We stopped outside the chapel, and Dad pointed out a line of gargoyles jutting out from the roof of the nave.

'See those. The originals wore away, so they modelled the replacements on the college First Eight after a heavy night in the bar of the Junior Common Room.'

'Really?'

'No of course not. Come on, we can look down on them from the top.'

The key was longer than my hand. The air smelt musty when I opened the low arched door to the tower. A row of lights flickered on as promised, revealing a formidable flight of narrow stairs with no handrail. I made Dad go first in case he toppled backwards. We crawled up the gritty steps, pausing frequently for a breather, and I wished I'd suggested a stroll around the famous, and considerably less hazardous, Fellows Garden.

At last, after traversing a long and mercifully flat passage, and then twisting and turning higher and higher, we emerged through a door onto the roof. We squinted in the sudden brightness and gulped the fresh air from the breeze. The panorama was magnificent, with the university spread out on three sides. Dad had hardly got his breath back before he was pointing out the domed circular library.

'The Radcliffe Camera,' he said. 'Houses the Bodleian Library.'

'I know.' It'd got to be the most famous building in Oxford.

'The Sheldonian Theatre's behind it, to the left.'

Here, he told me, Mum had sung in a performance of Britten's *War Requiem*, conducted by the composer himself. Then, using his stick to make sure I could follow his precise line, he methodically named every honey-coloured college we could see across the city.

After ten minutes or so, he ran out of landmarks and stayed leaning on the parapet, gazing north over the city, quiet and still. I left him to his memories and looked south across the tranquil open space of Christ Church Meadow to where the river, the Isis, glinted in the sun under a cloudless blue sky.

Eventually, having checked that Dad had seen enough, I led the way down, the lights reassuringly switching themselves on section by section. Halfway across the single horizontal stage of our cool but largely airless journey, we were startled by a soprano voice floating up from far below. I realised we were standing above the roof of the nave, exactly in the centre. As the sound soared, I understood why experts praised this chapel's acoustics so highly, with its choral evensong featuring regularly on Radio 3. Suddenly, the singer stopped, and I could just make out somebody speaking.

'Must be choir practice,' I whispered.

Dad nodded, then the same voice spiralled up again, repeating the bars we'd already heard. Another soprano joined in, followed by another and another and then the altos, the tenors and basses and, finally, the organ thundering. I stood transfixed, unable to make out any words, but swallowed up in the music as if I were part of it. The lights clicked off and we were left with a faint glimmer from a gap along the top of the wall to our left, which must have been how the sound was reaching us from the chapel floor. High in the confined passageway, every massive piece of masonry hewn by hand and hauled up here six centuries earlier, we stayed as still as the stones themselves, listening for a few minutes until, abruptly, the unseen celestial choir stopped. The organ's deep bass notes reverberated before fading slowly away, leaving this ancient place once more in silence.

I heard Dad take a deep breath. When I moved, the lights jerked back on, and I saw him leaning heavily on his stick with both hands. I stepped across and carefully lifted off his glasses before pulling his fastidiously folded handkerchief from his top pocket. Then, with the sound of the soprano rising once again, I dabbed away his tears.

The Party and the Pie

Peter Storey

A pair of friends had but one pie and cut it into two,
And this was very well until along came Kangaroo.
Their Australasian friend made three – and so they cut to
    thirds –
Which worked out very nicely 'til along came all the birds.

The Osprey and the Falcon were the first ones to arrive,
And the party now decided that the pie be cut in five.
But when the Starling, Thrush, and Kite flew down, though
    somewhat late,
T'was universally decreed the pie be cut in eight.

Two Pigeons joined the gathering: the pie was cut in ten,
And when the Dove and Sparrow joined, they cut it up again.
But, knowing that a smaller slice was better for his health,
The first one of the pair of friends was happy with a twelfth.

The second friend was not so very happy with his fate,
And then a Swallow Flock arrived – in number eighty-eight!
And taking pie division to a quite extreme extent,
The pie was cut to slices of a mere one percent.

The first friend though was happy that so many came to join;
He regaled them with his stories from the *Battle of the Boyne*.
The second friend just hoped that no more guests came from
    the air,
And t'was just as well they didn't: there was no pie left to
    share.

The Boy who Fell out of the Tree

Penny Frances

It was one of those November afternoons where the moist air hung fresh in his breath. Guff enjoyed the squish of his boots in the soggy humus, drip of water onto the fallen leaves. He liked the mouldy dankness, and the wet kept *them* away. Still, he had to keep his wits about him as he poked through the undergrowth, extracting the sodden takeaway cartons, rusty cans and slimy plastic bags with the grabber contraption on the end of his picking stick. He could lift and dump into the rubbish compartment of his shop-for-life bag without getting his hands dirty, and most days, there'd be something to treasure.

He rested against the trunk of a sweet chestnut, looking up through the lurid shine of thinning leaves. All quiet apart from the distant murmur of traffic, the drip of rain. This time of year, they kept indoors. *Them*, with their sudden movements and contempt in their eyes, scattering rubbish and laughing at his keep-safes. They shrank him to a wisp of himself, blown away on their scorn. He had to be wary, but now he allowed himself to drift and ponder on the glossy bark of the young sycamores looking just as if they'd had a fresh coat of Cuprinol, their leaves spotted from the splash of the brush.

He thought it was a squirrel, the scrabble through the treetops. Too heavy for a squirrel – a cat perhaps. Then, a crash and the thing falling: he felt his legs move forward, his arms stretch out as the force of the thing threw him backwards, his boots slipping their grip, nothing to break his fall as he landed smack on his backside. The breath was knocked out of him as the thing rolled to the ground.

Silence. That moment when the air settles back to its stillness. He twitched his long legs in their yellow cords. So far so... the old bones served him well. But what in hell's name? He hauled himself up to lean on his elbow.

It lay face down and motionless in the leaf mould. One of them hoodies – big ginger curls peeping out from the edges. Sharp shoulder blades poking the material; dirty thin legs in short khaki trousers; odd socks and one shoe missing. Guff reached for his stick and gave the thing a poke. It jerked into movement as if he'd given it an electric shock, then lay stock still again. He shuffled himself a bit closer and pushed to turn it over. As it rolled, it sat up with a jolt, and Guff shrank back.

This one had grey eyes like pools in a narrow pale face. The hood had fallen down, and the whiskey-coloured curls shone like the leaves.

Guff pulled himself up on his stick, his back creaking as it unwound.

'You're old Trash Can, aren't you? That's what they call you?'

Guff took a step back. 'Falling out the sky like a bad angel,' he muttered.

'What you got in your sack today then, Trash?' The creature crawled to Guff's bag and pulled it towards him.

Guff felt the blood beat in his head. This one was a lot smaller than the others, and on his own besides. Guff still towered a good six-feet-three, had his stick and all. But you couldn't use the stick, you couldn't touch the blighters. He looked up into the tree canopy to be sure there were no more. But he hadn't seen this one, had he?

'I'm not going to nick it off you, am I?' The boy was up, holding out the bag. Too quick in his movements. Like the others. 'Go on, take it.'

Guff grabbed at the bag, held it to him. Turned to walk up

to the path.

'I've seen you loadsa times from up in the trees. Mum calls me Monksey cos me dad's name was Monks, but it suits me, don't it?' The boy hopped along pulling on his shoe as he went.

Guff tried to hurry, but the boy skipped through the leaves beside him. He wasn't used to them chattering like this.

'I hide in the trees and watch. I saw that lot scare you, emptying your bag.'

'You talk a lot for a monkey. You want to be careful in them trees, could've killed the pair of us.'

Guff felt the dull pain in his coccyx from where he fell, slowing his pace.

'I was seeing if I could get from one tree to the next. I nearly did it too. Lucky you were there, init?'

'Lucky for you,' Guff muttered, taking a sharp turn left to shake the boy off, but Monksey scampered round to skip beside him again.

'Haven't you got a home to go to?' Guff asked.

'You see that first gate there, the green one?' He pointed to a row of dilapidated gates backing onto the edge of the woods. 'That leads to our house. We moved in the basement last summer.'

Guff stopped, gestured towards the gate with his stick. 'Time you went back there, then.'

'Next time I see them giving you hassle, I'll drop down on top of them, shall I? Give them a fright, shall I?'

'I can look after myself,' Guff said, but he couldn't help looking round. What if this one was a decoy?

'You should learn to climb the trees too. It's safest up there.'

'You'd be safest back home with your mother. Go on, scarper.' Guff stooped to brush the dirt off his trousers; they'd need a good wash now.

'Me mum's asleep, I can stop a bit longer.'

Guff turned to meet the boy's gaze. Those great eyes, taking everything in. Took him straight to a memory he didn't want. He had to look away.

'What do you do with all that rubbish?' The boy gestured towards the bag.

Guff tightened his grip on it, started walking on again. The boy scuttled alongside.

'I said I'm not going to nick it, am I?'

'It's criminal the waste,' Guff muttered. 'Take it home, make use of what I can, burn the rest.'

'Any treasure in there today?'

'You'll not be interested.'

'Show me.' Monksey tugged at Guff's sleeve.

Guff jerked his arm up to throw him off and the bag nearly hit the boy in the face. The two of them froze for a moment.

'I only want to see.' The boy's wide eyes filling.

Guff felt a hot wave of shame, didn't know what to do with it. The memory pressing harder now. His mother face down on the floor when he came in from school.

'Do you want to see my treasure?' the boy asked.

Guff looked down at the questioning face. His mother's black hair spread over the red carpet, that sour smell as he pushed at her, her face chalk white. He couldn't wake her. He thought she was dead.

'I'll show it you, I don't mind.' The boy started riffling through his trouser pockets. 'It's here somewhere.'

'I don't need to see your treasure any more than you do mine,' Guff tried.

Monksey pulled some dirty tissue and a few coins from his pocket. He looked up at Guff, his lip quaking like fear.

'It's not there. Where's it gone?' He jerked his head around, as if expecting his treasure to fly by.

'Put that stuff down and have another look.' Guff guided the boy to a fallen tree trunk.

The boy pulled his pockets inside out, held them like outstretched wings as he scuttled round, kicking up the leaves.

'Look, nothing, it's gone.'

'Perhaps you didn't have it when you came out.'

'I did. I remember feeling it when I was up the trees. You know when something's that smooth you have to rub it on your cheek to test the smoothness?'

'You may have dropped it when you fell. What is it, this bit of treasure?'

'It's the smoothest white – I hold it and let my fingers follow how it curves.'

'Like a piece of bone, then?'

Guff gave the boy the bits for his pockets and led him back the way they'd come. He used his stick to trace their path, looking down for something smooth and white.

'You can smell the sea on it, like the sea's bashed it to this roundness in your hand. If I've lost it, I don't know what I'll do.'

'We'll find it, don't worry.' Guff kept his eyes on the path. Not much white about, you'd think they'd spot it. Whatever the blazes it was.

'Where did you come across this object then?'

'I found it at the bottom of my mum's jewellery box. She gave me a right rollicking for going through her stuff. I hate upsetting me mum.'

His mother slapped him for causing the fuss, getting the neighbour involved. Guff learned to keep quiet after that, keeping to his room and his bottle top collection while his father came in from work. Until that time when he didn't, she didn't...

'But then she let me have it anyway,' the boy continued. 'She said me dad had given it her, the only thing she had of him. My dad was a free spirit, you see?'

'I'd give him free spirit,' Guff muttered, the memory tightening in his chest.

He walked on counting his breath in line with his steps. Told himself, this boy was nothing to do with it.

Then he spotted the sweet chestnut where Monksey had fallen on top of him. 'This is where you landed. Let's have a scout around.'

Monksey got down on his hands and knees, circling the area, while Guff picked away at the leaf mould with his stick. They searched in silence, just the rustle of leaves, the squish of his feet. Guff pulled out a couple of slimy crisp packets, turned over some stones, but nothing fit the description. He walked back a few yards to sit on a fallen log while the boy kept up his frantic scrabbling, like a dog after a buried bone.

'Hey, Monksey, lad,' Guff called to the boy. 'Come and take a break for a minute.'

Monksey looked up from his crouch position but didn't move. Guff opened the treasure compartment of his bag, pulled out the bicycle pedal wrapped in the old cloth and pretended to be absorbed in placing it carefully on the log beside him, smoothing out the rag. He could hear the boy approaching, but didn't look until he was right by him.

'Sit down, lad.' Guff pointed to the log the other side of the pedal. 'I was just checking what I found today.'

He pulled the rag aside to show the treasure. The boy bent to look at it.

'It's an old-fashioned steel one. See those spiky bits to give it grip?' Guff rubbed at the side with his cloth. 'It'll polish up nice, that will.' He handed it to Monksey.

'What'll you do with it?' The boy studied the thing as if it really were treasure.

'I'll find a place for it,' Guff said, thinking of the cabinets lining his living room. He pulled out the broken key ring, his other find from today.

'This is a piece of trash, really, but it'll look pretty enough with the other dangly bits.' He held up the pink plastic heart on a bit of chain. 'Some little lass will be missing that; at least I can take care of it.'

The boy stared at the key ring. Neither of them spoke for a moment as the trinket dangled between them.

'You'll find your treasure object at a time you're not looking for it. But you should be going home, lad. Your mother will worry when she wakes.'

Monksey kicked at the leaves in front of him.

'Hey, can I have a go with your stick for a minute? I need to look over there.' He pointed at a group of trees on the other side of the path.

Guff looked at the boy. Those dirty knobs of knee sticking out from the too short trousers.

'Is your mother poorly, lad?'

Monksey jumped up and backed away a few yards. Glared at Guff. 'There's nothing wrong with me mum,' he said, his voice shaking.

Guff pulled himself up and walked towards the boy.

'Here.' He handed the boy his stick. 'You squeeze the handle like that. Have a look for a minute, then I have to go.'

He sat back down and watched as the boy poked about in the undergrowth, pulled out a wodge of soggy newspaper.

'Just leave it in a pile, we'll put it in my bag then.' Guff called to him.

You could see the knobbles of the boy's backbone through the grey of his jumper. But Guff was getting himself carried away, asking about his mother like that, all because of the memory. He'd send the boy on his way in a minute. He wrapped the pedal in its bit of rag and placed it with the key ring back in the bag.

He looked up just in time to see the boy disappear through the trees towards the road. The lay-by.

'Hey,' Guff hurried after him, waving his arm, his heart pounding. To let the boy so near... what was he thinking?

'Wow!' The boy stopped dead in his tracks when he saw the outfit waiting in the lay-by. Guff couldn't help a wave of pride seeing the glint of polished chrome, the curve of the sidecar glistening with the fine drops of moisture. And the look on the boy. Those eyes wider than ever, and the open mouth threatening to split through the pale narrow face. Not a hint of scorn about him.

'It's like Wallace and Grommit. Never seen one of them before.'

'It's a Ural 750 Russian military sidecar outfit.' Guff moved round to pat the side of the shiny black tank. 'It's like what you see in the old war movies, they'd have a machine gun mounted just here.' He pointed to the front of the sidecar.

'Where's the gun? Have you still got the gun?'

'No,' Guff laughed. 'Wouldn't be a bad idea for frightening off the varmints, eh?'

The boy grinned. Guff unclipped the sidecar cover and carefully settled his bag in there.

'It's come down in the world now, just transporting my rubbish, you see?'

'It's beautiful,' said the boy.

There was a faint glint of late afternoon sun now, and Guff could feel the warmth on his back as he watched the light pick out the shine of the outfit and the line of the boy's cheekbone. He'd have been about this kid's age when his uncle took him to that motorcycle show soon after the war. The rows of gleaming handlebars, the smart little sidecars setting off a longing in him. But it was only a couple of years ago that he saw the Ural parked on the street with a 'For Sale' sign. He'd just got the grant for his furniture after the Council gave him his bungalow. He'd bought the outfit instead and scavenged the furniture.

'Will you take me for a ride in it?' The boy turned to look at Guff, his smile so winning that Guff knew it was all he wanted in the world; to seat the boy's scrawny body snug in the sidecar, kick the bike into action and putter noisily down the road. When they got home, he could make hot chocolate and show him the bird skulls, the bit of rusty shell, the key ring collection.

Guff opened the sidecar boot and took out a piece of rag. There might be room for the bag in there; he didn't gather that much today. He left the boot open and went to get the bag from the sidecar. The boy edged closer, anticipation nearly bursting out of him. Guff picked up the bag and gave the seat a quick wipe with the cloth. Looked back at the boy who took another step towards the sidecar.

Something in that wide-eyed eagerness. Guff knew in that instant he had to pull back.

'I'm sorry lad,' his voice croaky. 'I'd love to take you, that's the truth, but you know I can't, don't you?'

The boy ran his finger over the mudguard. 'Your biggest treasure?' He looked up at Guff.

Guff looked away. 'It is, but you must know. Hasn't that mother of yours taught you anything?'

'I told you, there's nothing wrong with me mum,' the boy snapped. He walked round stroking the outfit. Stopped with his back to Guff and fiddled about in the gutter with the stick.

'You should be getting back, lad,' Guff said to break the awkwardness.

Monksey turned around. His pale face was streaked with grey tear trails. It went through Guff to look at him.

'You get off home now. You may even find your treasure there after all.'

Monksey pulled his lips into a straight-lined smile. 'When I find it, do I get to go in your sidecar?'

'We'll see.'

But Guff knew he wouldn't be back in these woods. Not now. He felt in his bag for the plastic heart key ring, polished it on his bit of rag.

'Here, take this for your mother. Tell her you found it here.'

Monksey took the key ring and dangled it to catch the light. He wiped his face with his sleeve, and then he looked up and smiled.

'Thanks.' He clasped his hand round the treasure, turned and made his way back into the woods.

The Specific Ocean

Corinna Keefe

I was strolling along Dale Road one morning when I almost tripped and fell into the sea.

It had rained the night before, and I'd stepped over several puddles already, trying to keep my battered brown shoes clean. But this was different: a faint white edge betrayed the presence of brine. A breeze ruffled the two metre-square surface of the water and filled my lungs with cool salt air.

There was a seagull sitting on the far edge of the sea – the puddle – looking embarrassed. It mewed half-heartedly.

'I don't suppose you can explain this, can you?' I asked. It turned its feathered back on me.

I edged closer, half-expecting the ground to fall away, or the seascape to resolve into one of those chalk pictures with odd perspective. It remained solid, but my shoes slid around in the fine white sand. A wave crashed onto the shore a few inches in front of me. I stooped to wet my fingers, and then taste, in case the seagull and the smell and the breeze had all somehow arrived through separate means–

No.

Unmistakably salt. Unmistakably sea.

I straightened up slowly and glanced around. No one was in sight, which meant that no one had witnessed me grubbing around at the edge of the sea. Puddle, I mean. It had to be a puddle.

I walked around it with my face averted and went home by a different route.

When I set out for my walk the next day, I decided not to go anywhere near Dale Road. And yet somehow, I found myself slowly pacing up the hill again.

Perhaps it was not such a bad thing. Once I was there, I would see straight away that the sea had just been a puddle all along. I would feel a little silly and go home at peace.

But as I reached the crest of the hill, I realised that I was not alone. The two-metre patch of salt water was still there, and on one side, bridging the pavement and the road, was a large red-and-white striped deck chair with an old woman lying in it.

She was wearing a sensible skirt, jumper and shoes, and her hands were folded across her stomach. Her eyes were closed as if sunbathing.

I eyed her cautiously as I stooped down to check the water.

'It's still salt, you know. No change,' she said calmly.

I stepped backwards quickly.

'It doesn't make any sense,' I said.

'What doesn't?'

'This – this puddle! It shouldn't be salt!'

'And what about the seagull?'

I looked around wildly. How did she know about the seagull?

'He's under my chair,' she said. 'I always bring a few bits of bread for him, bless him. He gets a bit hungry when it's first settling in.'

'When what's settling in?'

'Why, the Ocean. When the Ocean arrives somewhere new, the fish are a bit shy for a while.'

'Why are you saying it like that?'

'Saying what like what?'

'The Ocean – like it has a capital letter. It's just a puddle! It's too small to be an ocean, or an Ocean!'

Finally, she opened her eyes and craned her neck to look directly at me.

'But it is an Ocean. And of course, it's small. Not all oceans have to be like those great big messes slopping about on the continental shelves. If it were that big, it wouldn't be the Specific Ocean.'

I gaped at her.

'You're mad,' I said at last. 'I hope someone comes and takes you home before your deckchair gets run over,' and I stomped off down the road.

'I know sarcasm when I hear it, old man!' she yelled after me.

On the third day, I decided not to take my walk at all. I kept myself busy and didn't even sit down for some coffee until after five o'clock, far too late for a walk.

I took my usual seat by the window overlooking the high street. I was halfway through a book, but it soon dropped to my lap while I gazed through the glass at the sun setting over the quiet town.

Except, I noticed with some annoyance, it was *not* quiet. The shops were closed, and the schools had let out long ago, but the streets seemed even busier than before. Several people were carrying towels rolled up under their arms. One man was quite definitely wielding an inflatable flamingo.

I don't know what got into me then. I flung the window open and stretched my head perilously out.

'Hey! Hey! What's happening?'

The man with the flamingo looked up and waved his pink companion cheerfully by one leg.

'We're having a beach party! Bring a few drinks if you're coming. Everyone's invited.'

'A beach party?' I said.

But he was already gone.

I resolved that I would march straight up the hill and confront the little old lady. Somehow – I could work out the details later – some way, she had filled the top of Dale Road with water and caused a public disturbance. Well, I would tell her where she could trickle off to, and her tame seagull too.

As soon as I stepped outside, I found myself in the middle of a chatting, swarming tide of people. There were young children in pushchairs, teenagers already in their swimming costumes, parents with beach bags slung over their shoulders. It was uncharacteristically warm for the time of year, with a hint of salt and smoke that caught at the back of my throat.

As I turned the corner into Dale Road, my heart sank. The shore of the Ocean was already completely obscured by beach umbrellas. Somebody was grilling sausages in the distance.

I caught a glimpse of red-and-white canvas and marched over to the old lady's deckchair. She was sitting up with the seagull on her shoulder, smiling and greeting everyone who passed.

'What on earth do you think you're doing?'

'Why, I'm enjoying an evening at the beach.'

'And what about all these other people?' I demanded.

'They're enjoying themselves too.'

'They are making a mess. They are making a noise.' I had to raise my voice to be heard. 'They are blocking a public highway!'

The old lady looked calmly up and down the street.

'I don't see any cars trying to pass through here just now, lovey. Everyone's coming for the Ocean. Why don't you go for a swim?'

'I'm not going to do that!' I raged. 'I'm not going to make *myself* ridiculous just because *you* have some ridiculous idea that you're running some kind of public service–'

'I'm not running it,' the old lady interrupted me. Her tone had become rather steely. 'You keep talking about the Ocean like it needs planning permits and supervision and God knows what else. It's the Ocean.'

'Then who's supposed to be in charge? Who's going to supervise all these swimmers? What if–'

'Look–'

'Stop interrupting me!'

She laughed. People had started to gather round, but she remained as still in her chair as ever. She didn't seem bothered by other people at all.

'Look here. The Ocean exists. You can't do anything about it. These people are enjoying themselves. You can't really do anything about that either. You got here too late.'

I stared at her in silence. I hated her.

'Join in,' she said, kindlier. 'You can go home, or you can join in.'

I went home.

I slept badly that night and woke up in the kind of mood where one drops things all the time. I smashed a coffee cup and spilt cereal on the floor.

Beach-goers! I thought, wielding the dustpan and brush with vicious concentration. People who thought that it was perfectly reasonable to circumnavigate an ocean on their way to work. Silly people. People who grilled sausages in the street. People who carried around inflatable flamingos. Fly-tippers. The kind of people whom the *neighbourhood* needed to *watch*!

The window still hung open where I had leant out the night before. There was a little wind, but it was quite different now; the air seemed stale and thin. A dirty paper plate skittered down the street. A plastic bag sagged against a lamp post.

I looked down at the shards of the cup scattered across the floor in a puddle of rapidly cooling coffee. I looked at the pan and brush in my hands – anaemic, dusty hands. I hadn't made time for holidays. I thought of the old lady's hands, brown and wrinkled, curled tightly in her lap. I wondered how much more rubbish must be strewn around the beach.

With a sigh, I swung my coat on over my red-and-white

striped pyjamas. I stuffed a roll of black bin bags into my pocket, slipped on a pair of shoes, and set out once again for Dale Road.

The beach was almost invisible under a thick snow of paper napkins, plastic forks, deflated beach balls, mysteriously abandoned shoes, cigarette butts, soft drink bottles, and plastic cups.

'At least they were enjoying themselves,' I said aloud. With a sigh, I got to work.

I had been picking up debris for perhaps half an hour when I lifted a napkin and saw the lady smiling up at me. She had been quite buried.

'Good morning,' she said.

'Good morning,' I said, shortly. Then: 'I'm sorry.'

'I'm glad you're here,' she replied. 'I hoped you would come back.'

'I didn't want you to be left up here on your own,' I said, feeling rather foolish. 'I mean I – I didn't think it was fair that you should have to clean up on your own.'

'Well, I think I might walk into town and get us a cup of tea. Do you mind finishing up?'

'Not at all,' I said. I brushed a few more scraps of rubbish aside, and she levered herself stiffly up out of the deckchair.

'I'll be back soon,' she said.

'No rush,' I said.

After 45 minutes, there were six fat, black rubbish bags sitting by the side of the road. The beach remained quiet, even though it was a baking hot day. I'd discarded my coat long ago. There was still no sign of the old lady.

I undid the buttons of my pyjama shirt and hung it carefully over the deckchair. I rolled my pyjama trousers tightly up to the knee and kicked off my shoes.

The first touch of the waves against my toes was like the

first sip of water after a long, desperate night. I felt the ripples spread out calmly across my mind. I shuffled forward, sighing as the sand caressed my feet, pieces of shell and sea-glass turning up to glint in the morning light. There was a bubbling white edge of foam to the waves which bounced up at me in greeting. The sun scattered off the water in a thousand tiny dawns.

I walked out until the water was chest-deep and dove into the arms of the Ocean. It was cool, so deliciously cool after working in the heat and muck. Tiny currents clasped my hands. Salt water flowed over my face, and I opened my eyes. It was quite clear.

My feet groped for the ocean floor and found smooth rock. Little fish flocked around my ankles. Above me, light flickered through the greenish water, and sunbeams reached down like the columns of some vast hall. I swam in and out of them, marvelling.

The Specific Ocean stretched around me, above me, in fathomless depths and distances which had been invisible from the surface. It was a whole world – a whole specific world – vast, tiny, and everywhere unmistakably itself.

When at last I came to the surface, I kicked up my legs and lay on my back, arms spread wide. The waves moved gently against my side, and I turned diagonally to the tide so that I could lie still. I heard the seagull cry in the distance.

After a long time, someone called out:

'Hello!'

I paddled myself upright and looked toward the shore, shading my eyes with one hand. It was the lady, clutching a small brown paper bag.

'Hello! I've brought you tea! And a Chelsea bun!'

'I'll come right out!' I shouted back and began to swim. I pulled and kicked in a steady breaststroke, feeling stronger than I had in years. Salt water was meant to be good for the health, I remembered.

'Did you have a good swim?' said the old lady.

'I certainly did, thanks,' I said. 'And thanks for the tea.'

'It's just the thing after being in the water,' she said. 'Myself, I like to swim first thing in the morning. It gets cold in winter, but they say it keeps you young. And a hot flask of tea will set you up for the day afterwards.'

I sat on the sand beside her deckchair while we ate in companionable silence. I amused myself by throwing crumbs of Chelsea bun for the seagull to fetch.

'May I ask you something?' I said, eventually.

'Of course.'

'How – how long does the Ocean usually stay? In one place, I mean?'

She leant back in her deckchair and stared thoughtfully at the sky.

'Depends where the Ocean feels at home, feels welcome. It usually likes to move on after a storm. Storms shake things up, like.'

'Did you come here after a storm?'

'After many storms,' she said, and laughed to herself.

'Do you get tired of it?'

'Of the Ocean? No. But I do get tired of moving, sometimes.'

'Do you think you'll ever stop?'

'This has been a lot more than one question.'

I nodded. Stretched. Stood up.

'I think it's time I ought to be moving off myself.'

'Will you come again tomorrow?' she said. She looked worried, suddenly.

'I'm not sure. I'll see how things go.'

'All right,' she said. Her cramped hands twisted nervously in her lap. 'Be seeing you, then.'

I hesitated.

'Look, I don't know about tomorrow. But if you should need

anything – I live down on New Street. Number 84. There's a spare key under the doormat.'

She looked up at me with relief.

'Thank you.'

'Be seeing you,' I said hastily and left.

There was a strange wind at my back as I walked down Dale Road. By the time I reached the house, thick black clouds were gathering. I shivered in my damp pyjamas and made sure the shutters were closed before I went to bed.

The storm raged for two days and two nights. Those same black clouds unleashed the heaviest rain in years, and gale-force winds ripped around the corners of the streets. Warnings came in over the radio and television telling everyone to stay indoors and get animals under shelter.

I stayed in my sitting room, in an agony of worry about the lady and the Ocean. She would be quite exposed up there on the hill. Worst of all, she had said that the Specific Ocean often moved on after a storm. By the time it was safe to go outside, the Ocean might have disappeared altogether. I knew I would never find it again.

Early on the third day, I was woken by an unfamiliar silence. The rain had stopped, and the wind had gone down. Everything was quiet. I lay back for a second, relishing the peace; then I thought of the Ocean.

I flew out of bed and pulled on my clothes. I made a flask of hot tea in the biggest Thermos I could find. I looked in the biscuit tin and found a few stale ones left – those would do for the seagull.

I checked over the house thoroughly before I left. By some miracle, no tiles had come off and all the shutters stood firm. I closed the door behind me with a snap.

Some instinct made me check under the doormat. The spare key was still there, despite the storm. Just in case somebody should need it.

I set off up the hill at a run, the Thermos and biscuit tin banging around in my rucksack.

The Ocean was still there. It was. The waters seemed grey and muddier than before, with hanks of seaweed tossed up on to the surface, but they were still indisputably Ocean, just as they had been on that first day when I was so furiously reluctant to believe.

The sand was whipped up into dunes and wild shapes by the wind, and driftwood lay scattered along the shore. The deckchair was lying near the waterline, overturned on its side.

I approached it nervously, but it was empty. I felt enormously relieved, and for a second didn't know why, until the thought came into my mind: no body. Wherever the lady was, she was not here. She had found somewhere else to be.

I felt something pecking hopefully at my feet. It was the seagull. I turned the deckchair right-side up and sat down in it gently. Slowly, trying not to startle the bird, I took out the biscuit tin. I sprinkled a few crumbs on the sand at my feet.

'There you go, Mr Gull,' I said. I put my feet up and settled back into the chair.

I must have dozed off for a few minutes.

After so many days of rain and thunder, the sun felt unusually warm on my face. Hardly English at all. I opened my eyes and stretched luxuriously.

There the Ocean was, still breaking and chattering quietly by my side. The seagull had hopped up beside me and was busily clanging around in the biscuit tin. In the distance, I caught a glimmer of pink.

Over on the far side of the Specific Ocean, a flamingo was standing on one leg, peacefully snoozing.

Waiting for a Small Boat Coming in

Jennie Turnbull

I'm waiting for a small boat coming in.
Its sails are red, the hull is painted blue
and I'm hoping you'll be at the helm again.

I thought I saw you in a childhood dream,
on waves that rose to let the light shine through.
I'm waiting for a small boat coming in.

The sky is greening dark; it threatens rain.
A steady hand will keep the tiller true.
I'm hoping you'll be at the helm again.

Too many months, my patience wearing thin,
I scan the empty sea for red and blue.
I'm waiting for a small boat coming in.

Your absence has become my secret shame,
the burden that I carry overdue.
I'm hoping you'll be at the helm again.

I listen for your pebbles on the pane –
my cargo is your problem too.
I'm waiting for a small boat coming in,
and praying you'll be at the helm again.

I Was Walking Corso Magenta

Jonathan Parker

I was walking Corso Magenta
In Milan's light November rain.
Pallid yellow failing into grey
From Palazzo della Stelline to the
Crowded Bar Magenta.
Drinkers: drops spilling from
A discarded glass to coalesce
Into later evening damp.

I was thinking, let's walk by the sea again,
Once this is over, and I return.

No students now in Cattolica
Before the cruellest month.
The quadrant green but yet unrun;
Shrouded halls dispensing nought but
Silence, and graduating
A stopped, beating heart.

I was thinking, let's walk by the sea again,
Once this is over, and I return.

Evening deftly gentled;
Sant' Ambrogia – sleeping doctor
mummified – as vital as the masked living.
A quiet, unanticipated life dies,
And dies a little more.
I was thinking, let's walk by the sea again,
Once this is over, and I return.

The Flood

Xenobe Purvis

Given the choice between fire and water, most of us would choose water. Fire scalds: it smothers and spreads. Water is soft, a salve. It accommodates. That's what we thought, anyway, it's why we moved to that place at all: to be by the river. To see the calm green breadth of it every day of our lives.

Perhaps what we liked best about water is that we found it to be biddable: it fills a glass, it falls along a throat, it allows us to float on our backs in the bright height of summer, encircling our hot bodies, cooling us. But water isn't biddable. It isn't soft or accommodating. Water divides. It drowns. Sometimes it is lazy and sly, it wears you out so thoroughly that eventually you drown yourself.

The first sign of the flood was in Mrs Cobbold's house, the one right beside the river. She went down to her cellar to fetch some more cat food and found a rippling floor of water, ankle-height, where no water used to be. It'll subside, we told her later, but by the following morning, it had reached all of our basements, and, by that afternoon, it was at our ground floors. We watched, aghast, as the murky water surrounded our television sets. It stained the fabric on our sofas, floral patterns ringed with rising green. Our dogs were lifted off the floor; they paddled now instead of walking. Our children smacked flat palms on the surface. They scooped up flotsam: photo frames, cushions, pens. Some of us tried to shift the water with buckets, but the more we threw into the hedges outside, the more seemed to swell into our sitting rooms.

Mr Strout's house is a little higher than the rest; we gathered there to discuss the water. Some of us tried to place blame.

'The water is rising', we said, 'because of us. We treated the water blithely for so long, and now it's taking over our homes.'

'Don't be silly', some of us rejoined, 'this has nothing to do with us. And anyway, there's no point in looking backwards. We need to look forwards. We need a plan.'

The plan we came up with, the only plan our dazed minds could alight on, was to wait. We would wait to see if the water diminished.

For a day or so, the water stayed level. It didn't leave, but it didn't rise either, lapping gently against our kitchen cabinets. We might almost have got used to it: wading in wellington boots to make our meals; living on our upper floors. But then it started rising again, and that was when the trouble really started.

The problem, you see, was that this time, the second time, a rumour circulated right after the water rose. Someone swore that he saw a group of teenagers – the Paget boy and the Sutton brothers – standing at the banks of the river the evening before. They were doing something there, we heard. Some sort of mischief. As a result of their mischief, the water began to grow again – that was the rumour, anyway.

The first division was created among us: between those who wanted to punish the boys, and those who sought to spare them.

In the end, we arrived at a compromise: we would impose a curfew. Everyone would be confined to their homes as soon as the sun went down. This idea didn't last long. People were angry: why should everyone be punished for the mischief of three teenagers? In the middle of the night, the Paget boy went missing. Was he taken, we wondered? Or did the river claim him?

Some of us searched for him, but most of us were so fixated on the water pooling within our homes, rising up our patterned wallpaper and filling the interior of our grandfather clocks, that we did nothing for him. The water smelled of something. It didn't have the river's smell, that deep green scent, wet and heady. Instead, it smelled extremely sweet with an acrid after-taste, like burning sugar. It sickened some of us, but several thought the strange sweetness was a sign: this wasn't a normal flood, it was a blessing. Something good would follow.

Mr Strout's house was still relatively untouched, and so we met there once again to deliberate. Some of us had strange things to report: the water was pinkening, they said. It was changing colour. Some said they saw fish swimming in it, large silver scales brushing against the carpet. Some said they had tasted the water. It was delicious. It had a curiously calming effect, they told us.

It was still summer at that point, and so the sweet-smelling, pinkening water didn't chill us. We were glad to see it each morning as we made our way downstairs. It cast its spell. By then, we'd all started drinking it, just a sip here and there. It made each day a bit brighter. Even Mrs Paget, sleepless and wild, found herself soothed by the water. When we spent time in it, our skin felt fresh and smooth. Wrinkles were ironed out of our bodies, grazes were healed. Congestion, aches, gas – all of our ailments began to disappear.

The water stayed level, as high as our waists, for several weeks. It swirled down the high street, gathering litter and leaves. It found its way into every hole and crevice, all the nests and warrens. Wading along, we would often meet the floating carcasses of small, drowned voles, the bloated bodies of rats. The ants retreated from it in thick determined lines, which was strange, we thought, because ants like sweet things. The water was getting sweeter and redder every day.

Now people were travelling to witness it, strangers from other places queueing to see the spectacle, our Venice filled with magic canals. Some of us didn't like that, of course. The crowds coming in, bringing greedy mouths to our precious supply of pink water. Fights began to break out: scuffles, small flares of irritation. We put Mrs Cobbold in charge of issuing tickets. She seemed to like the job, the power to decide who could experience the water and who could not.

It was only a matter of time before somebody drowned. When our gardens and homes were filled with water, and we were stumbling around in an intoxicated haze, it's no surprise that someone eventually succumbed to the flood. Mrs Riley, it was, young and newly married. We watched her sink quietly into the water, the surface barely rippled. Strange what little response this evoked. We stared at the water for a long time, then continued with our business.

Her husband, Mr Riley, felt differently. He hated the water, he told us; he punched it with balled fists, he kicked it, he swore. It offended us, the way he spoke about our beloved flood. We watched his blood blend with the reddened water around him. His body circled aimlessly on the surface for a few hours, then sank out of sight somewhere downstream.

By then, the water had displaced many parts of our lives. We no longer ate; we drank insatiably instead. We rarely slept; we swam. We didn't laugh, or cry, or even speak. We were lulled into nothingness, into sweet oblivion. Most of us, that is: the water didn't have the same effect on Mr Strout. The flood had never really reached his house, and he'd made a point of staying away from it.

One day, he came down towards our flooded plain, dragging a rowing boat behind him. Despite the heat, he'd wrapped a scarf around his face. He wore rubber gloves on his hands and high waders on his legs. He eyed the water with distrust. He seemed afraid of it; he was determined not to let it meet his skin. He began to row, his oars touching our bodies while we swam beside him.

He surprised us: he tried to lift us into the boat. One by

one, his rubbered hands reached for us. Some of us allowed ourselves to be lifted – we all liked Mr Strout, and he seemed so keen to get us out of the water, it felt rude not to do as he directed. But some of us resisted. There was a fierceness in his face that frightened us. Once we were out of the water, we feared Mr Strout wouldn't let us back in.

He took some of us up to his house. Most of us. It took hours. He ferried boatloads of blinking, unspeaking people up the hill. Some found it so odd to be back on land again that they could barely walk. He carried them or looped a thin arm around their backs to support them. He's old, Mr Strout. He looked tired, but he didn't stop until he'd gathered everyone he could. The ones who went with Mr Strout didn't come back.

For a while, it felt strange without them. Quietness reigned: the sounds of our hometown, the usual background hum of people and lives, had been muffled entirely. It was eerie, the blanketing silence created by the flood. We wondered whether we should join Mr Strout and the others on the land. But then, to our amazement and delight, the water began rising again.

There was more water, much more, and fewer of us: we no longer worried about sharing it between us all. It absorbed our houses entirely, our cats and dogs and children, our bedrooms and belongings. We swam around our chimneys. We listened to the water lapping against the tiles of our rooves. We tangled ourselves in telephone wires.

We had never been happier. True, our numbers had now diminished. People disappeared frequently. One or two more swam in the direction of Mr Strout's and didn't return. Others simply went missing. We wondered vaguely if they'd swallowed too much and slipped beneath the surface. Sometimes it seemed as though we could feel their water-logged limbs brushing against our feet.

The water was no longer sweet and pink; at some point during those weeks (or was it months?), the water dimmed to wine-darkness and the taste began to burn. The bitterness took hold of our tongues. It was like drinking molten charcoal.

It was then that we noticed our population had dwindled to only two. Me and Mrs Cobbold. There she lay, stretching her satiated body along the uppermost branch of a tree. She sat up suddenly and swung her legs beneath her.

'You know what', she said. 'I don't like this anymore. Look at this place. It's ruined.'

'No,' I told her, 'not ruined, but bettered.'

She shook her head.

'I think I'll go to Mr Strout's. They might still be there. I don't want to stay here.'

'Stay,' I said.

She drifted away, and I was left alone. I wasn't lonely to start with. All the company I'd ever need was here in this flood. All the pleasure, all the rest. I could be content forever. But something wasn't right – something flickered at the back of my mind, teasing me, irritating me. I remembered that I had known people here and loved them. I remembered my home, the place where I had lived for so long. I remembered Mr Strout and Mrs Cobbold, even that Paget boy. I missed our life. I missed the 'we-ness' of our daily existence. I had wanted to live amphibiously, to commit myself to the water, but I knew now that my body couldn't tolerate it.

I willed the water to carry me upstream, but it would not. My arms grew tired. My throat was dry, my legs were weak. I said goodbye to the beguiling flood. I slipped beneath, but by then there was no one around to notice.

On Kerrera Island

Sharon Black

This morning, I'm hiking

in the hills of Andalusia, figs dripping
from the trees,

pomegranates splitting on hot limestone rocks
amid the scrub, miles from any road.

I'm striding, dusty,

beside a *Nationale*
somewhere in the *Midi*, my hitching thumb
hooked firmly round my rucksack strap,

I've dropped behind my friends
on Rannoch Moor, damp from sweat
and midge spray, ten miles in,

another six to reach our lodge
along the Way
that keeps dipping, re-emerging.

I'm everywhere I've ever
walked alone, exhausted, aching
with some twinge or injury

and nothing but to keep on walking,
until the rawness sings
more softly, each moment passing

to the next as the spirit disengages
from its capable machine,
pulse playing out

against a drop that could be anywhere,
each step any step, no difference
between a footfall and a life.

The Soul is a Separate Thing from the Body

Kate McCarthy

Two pairs of eyes searched the sky intently. They were both the very same shade of grey-blue, a reflection of the sea on this dreich spring day. One pair looked out from the bright, shining face of a small boy. Lachlan. He wore a hand-knitted jumper he had long outgrown, his pale wrists peeking out from the sleeves. The second pair looked out from lined, weather-beaten skin. Rows upon rows of miniature crevasses that widened and closed with every smile. Not that he smiled too often, mind, did Lachlan's grandfather. Angus. He was lean and wiry with an aquiline nose and a grey beard to hide the hollows in his cheeks. Lachlan's eyes were just like his father's, he'd been told.

Between the salt spray and the drizzle, there was no hope of staying dry. The air was thick with a fine mist that coated everything so that their eyelashes and the wool fuzz on their jumpers glittered. The small boat bobbed in the water, engine cut.

Lachlan searched his grandpa's face. This was his first time out catching birds. He was there to watch and learn. And, above all, to be quiet. He was trying hard to swallow down his words. He wanted to say 'look! Over there!' at an otter or a clump of floating seaweed or a technicolour buoy emerging from the fog. But his grandpa's expression was dour, carved in granite. Lachlan zipped his mouth shut, locked his voice up and threw the key over the side, imagining it making a soft landing on a sandbank below. Man and boy sat side by side on the narrow bench in silence, knock-knees bumping together.

Waves slapped over the weighted board submerged a few metres away.

Lachlan lived with his grandparents in a squat stone cottage twenty feet from the bay. In the time before he went to school, before his teachers punished the Gaelic out of him and the English into him, his grandpa was *seanair* and he was *ogha*, a *chuilein*, a *bhobain*. Grandson, my laddie, my rascal. His grannie told him old folk tales full of terror while she knitted in her favourite chair, a threadbare wingback that carried the memory of her shape. He'd sit in his rightful place opposite her, on a low chair with its legs sawn off, mug of warm cow's milk in hand, demanding another one, another one. Soft 'bh's and 'th's rolled out from her mouth and across the hearth, filling the little room with a susurration that rose and fell like a sea swell.

There once was a silver-haired selkie who lured young men out to sea, where they lived for a time in the land under the waves. Most were never seen again. Some were returned to the shore wrapped in reams and reams of shining green seaweed.

In the boat, after an undetermined period of time, Angus pointed up, holding a finger to his lips. 'Quiet now', he meant. A bird had appeared high in the brume above them, black wing tips cutting slowly through the air as if through treacle. Lachlan wanted to jump up and shout – A GANNET! – but instead gripped his grandpa's arm tight, transfixed by the creature. He knew that gannets had a six-foot wingspan, which was twice as wide as he was tall, and that they laid a single blue egg.

The bird caught sight of the bait fish shimmering a few inches below the surface. It began its descent, moving with the speed and force of an arrow. Two pairs of grey-blue eyes watched the same trajectory downwards, entranced. Then an awful, irrevocable thwack rang out. The boy flinched as it hit the board. His grandpa did not. The bird's neck was broken instantly. Grannie watched from the kitchen window, working a tea towel around a cup. The small, everyday sadness which had settled on her was visible as the merest furrowing of her brow.

Lachlan knew that his father had gone out to sea one day and never come back, though no one had thought to explain it to him further. He knew that his mother had died after that and gone to heaven, too. This much he knew. But he still had questions. What did she look like? What was his job? Could he whistle? Was she tall? Grannie was more inclined to talk but still evaded most of them, eyes always fixed on the bedlinen she was folding or the sink she was cleaning.

Grannie reminded him to include his ma and pa in his prayers every night at bedtime. She said that heaven was up in the sky, in the stars. Lachlan didn't notice the panicked glances between grown-ups when he wondered aloud about his parents, but he would remember for the rest of his life the time that Mary Mckinnon said that his mummy wasn't in heaven. Certainly not.

They motored back into the bay; the gannet tucked into the prow of the boat. Lachlan stared and stared. How plush his white breast was. How giant and out of place he seemed.

'Is he dead?'

His grandpa turned around, arm firmly on the rudder.

'Yes, Lachlan.'

'Are you sure he'll never wake up again?'

'I'm sure.'

'Like my mum and dad?'

Angus maintained his gaze towards the shore. The back of his head radiated implacable silence. There was only the sound of the boat slicing through spray, the engine purring out a low-pitched note. Lachlan reached out and stroked the bird's head with a heart-breaking lightness of touch.

At dusk, the ball of the sun dropped between two islands

far out at sea, cradled equidistantly between them. Feathers were strewn about the ground in front of the house, swirling in the wind.

Lachlan was asking how the bird could have gone to heaven when he'd seen it in the kitchen. Grannie looked across the water, wiping her hands on her apron. There were more and more of these questions now. She couldn't deny him forever.

'Well,' she started to say quietly, 'the soul is a separate thing from the body.'

Her whisper was swallowed up by rustling reeds which arched in the breeze. But Lachlan wasn't listening. He was busy collecting feathers into a bucket.

In the weeks that followed, the boy took to combing the beach. He was looking for slimy, green ribbons. He was looking for a supine body, wrapped up like a mummy with seaweed instead of bandages. He was looking for someone brought back by a selkie and left lying on the ridged sand at low tide.

He knew that his father had gone out to sea and never come back. He knew that his mother had followed soon after, gone to be with him. Grannie said they were in heaven, but Mary Mckinnon didn't think that was true. The body of the gannet was in a pot in the kitchen. Grannie said heaven was in the sky, but it felt quite obvious to Lachlan that his parents were under the water. Out at sea.

The land under the waves is revealed only on crystal clear days when the sea is like a millpond. On such days, it's hard to tell whether fishing boats float along the surface in our world or below it, in the land under the waves.

He imagined white-crested waves as the ceiling of the place where his parents now dwelt. When he went out on the boat with his grandpa and looked over the side, he saw his parents looking up as the hull sliced above their heads. He envisioned them finding the key he'd thrown overboard and swimming up, up, up, towards the dappled light, to give it back to him.

He gave up asking questions and took to sitting quietly by the window overlooking the bay. Quietness reigned in the little house. So many words with nowhere to go. Grannie had started knitting him a bigger jumper, her fingers frantic. His grandpa mended nets. Their time was always occupied, their hands always busy. This was the way they grieved their one son, only ever truly stilled by sleep.

Lachlan kept his grey-blue eyes on the water. In his mind, he visited another world where sunlight strained to reach him, and faraway sound was muffled. A gannet tucked back its wings and thwacked into the sea, disappearing into the land beneath the waves.

Thought -washing

Denise O'Hagen

There are no words for dawn, only
        For its effect on us. The winter light
Swilled, ink-blue morphing linen grey
        To white, soaking the thickened window pane,
The cracked seats of the London-to-Brighton train,
        My chapped hands, my feet; no stained-glass
Window ever streamed
        A light so sweet.

I hung out my rags of thoughts, freely
        In air before me – the maimed, the
Soiled and stained, and watched them sway
        In time with the train: the ghosts we carry,
So fretted and frayed, yet pressing through
        The solid people of this world.
And all the while,
        The white light shone.

And days later, I found
        I couldn't ignore myself any longer.
What we were was slowly disengaging itself
        From the idea of us: had you noticed?
I envied the lovers of literature;
        Romeo and Juliet never got to this point –
But they also were never gifted the chance
        To wash their thoughts clear in the light.

Conducting

Jack Fenton

She watched her mother collapse on top of the casket, her back heaving up like a piston. Her pin sprung from her lapel and landed in a bouquet of roses. Thomas the Tank Engine stared out at the audience, nestled in between red petals and green stalks.

Danielle wondered how the oak case felt; if it was like pressing your forehead against glass. Would it leave an imprint on her mother's face, tear stains forming a watercolour of muddied reds, blues and blacks?

The person stood behind her, a relative she had only seen at family gatherings, pushed forwards. She felt the sharp nose of his costume – the front of a train – poke into her spine.

Danielle looked down at her breast, emblazoned with a patch that read *train conductor*. The collar of her pressed shirt tightened around her neck. She had almost complained, then saw the sea of DIY trains and official merchandise as she arrived, and it died in her throat. She thought about the only other funeral she had been to – that of her grandmother, where everything was black and brooding.

The funeral director stood in the corner, his eyes scanning the room. Danielle kept watching him, waiting for a flutter of amusement to cross his face. Dressing as the Fat Controller was not, she imagined, part of his job description. As her mother started to cry, he had dipped his head, top hat drooping like a dying sunflower.

Danielle watched her mother be ushered away as her father whispered into her ear. She envisioned the blog post that would release in a few days, beamed out to her mournful followers. For once, there would be no hyperbole. The room erupted in murmurs as she departed. How brave they were, how much they'd suffered, how impressive and admirable this all was.

A smattering of commiserations echoed in Danielle's ears. The characters she had watched since she was a child sat beside her on rows of bone white chairs: James, Percy, Henry, Thomas. All crumpled and creased by slap-dash costumes and fumbled alterations in kitchens. But they were here. He would've loved that.

In a blink, she stood over the casket. The stench of acrylic paint struck her nostrils, and she dove her head towards the rose petals, the aroma soothing her goose-pimpled flesh. Thomas' face stared back at her. A few stray tear stains dotted his cheeks. The likeness was uncanny, and Danielle noted to write the artist a glowing review once everything had settled down.

In some ways, the train watching her was better than seeing her brother's face. What did he look like now? His cheeks must have sunk and turned sallow, his skin a greasy grey. His eyes, in her mind, would be open, staring at the inside of his tomb.

She pressed her hands onto the casket, fingertips gliding along the varnish. Her brother lay here. In a box fit for a child. Behind her, on the sixth row, little Percy exclaimed 'Choo Choo!'. A hush fell over the room. She debated slamming her fists onto the artwork, smashing the lid into splinters, and tearing off her uniform as she did so. From there, she would attack them all, ripping and scratching every reference to trains from the room until they were all naked and bare and actually real. But she didn't. She looked one final time; every fleck of paint interned to memory. As she moved off, she grasped the Thomas pin in between the stems and stuffed it into her pocket.

'See you around.'

In the evening, Percy rushed amongst tall legs and polished shoes, diving in between gaps of conversation.

'Who are you meant to be?' he asked. And with the smile you reserve for young children, they would say which character they were. When he approached Danielle, lips sticky with a lolly, she responded before he could say anything.

'Wow. A train conductor,' he said, 'Why didn't you lead Thomas in with everyone else?'

She drained the wine in her hand in one fluid shot. 'Because it wasn't my place. It's not what they wanted.'

Instead, her father and uncles had carried him, a fictional character lifted by four men cosplaying as train conductors. Three of them had cried. It had looked like a fetish event for a specific type of locomotive enthusiast, and it made her feel sick.

Dregs of crimson clung to the inside of her glass. Discussion swirled around the room. Weren't funerals meant to be reflective and quiet? Weren't they meant to be about remembrance?

There was a certain unease in how people spoke to her versus her parents. Towards them, peoples' voices were quiet and respectable, unscripted condolences offered with a tactile squeeze of their shoulders. But to her, there was rehearsed passion, an A level drama student trying to nail their performance in a school play.

'He had a good eighteen years,' one of her uncles had said, his neck crimson, empty glass dangling by his side, 'Partly because of you.'

Another, a woman she hadn't recognised, approached her and said, 'What you've done here is amazing.'

James, his favourite train, was painted onto her cheek. 'Harry would've loved it.'

At one point, an old woman had shuffled over to where she

was sat. She wore only a Thomas pin, crooked against her black blouse, and Danielle felt a sense of camaraderie for this woman she did not know.

'He'll be watching this up in heaven. God is with him now.' She had said.

This swished around in her head like the Vermouth in her topped up glass. She hadn't thought about where he had ended up. The idea of him in heaven made her snicker. Angels would escort him through the pearly gates, and then fail to get his attention as he zoomed along the tops of clouds. Train noises would bellow out of his mouth, thunderclaps in the sky. He'd look for a train set, which she was sure God would provide, and for the rest of eternity that would be his entertainment. Why would a God interest him when nothing else did?

Or maybe there was nothing. His consciousness had floated off into the sky, like the steam from a kettle. His body, all six feet of it, would lay in that box painted to look like the love of his life.

She thought of a greatest hits playlist – maybe his best experiences were replayed to him before he died. What would've been his favourite memory? Would it be when he was first introduced to trains? When a meltdown at age one was satiated by a small wooden toy with wheels he could spin. Would it be when one of the voice actors from the show sent a video for his sixteenth birthday? He had repeated the message verbatim every hour for a month. She wondered if she featured prominently in any of them, or whether she was always an accessory to his train-fuelled fever dreams.

Her mother brought her another glass of red wine. 'You're doing really well,' she said, in the voice she used for her Facebook videos. 'I'm proud of you.'

Danielle smiled back, her teeth stained purple, and gnawed on the inside of her cheek.

She had tried to slip outside when a relative – a second cousin – had grabbed her by the arm.

'I've not seen you since you were this high,' he gestured and bellowed a laugh.

Danielle smiled but said nothing.

'You're doing your A Levels now, right? How are they going?'

Better than her GCSE's had. A time period punctuated by weekends spent chugging more coffee than a sixteen-year-old should ever consume. Evenings of scribbled notes on *Frankenstein* and *Of Mice and Men*, spider diagrams diagnosed a different colour for each concept. She'd contort her face and point it towards the paper, demanding the words fall from her ears and scatter onto the pages. What appeared instead were trains.

Their names, their weight, their make, their accents. A Yorkshire man, a Scottish woman. Their garbled dialogue and lavish design blocked everything else out. The blank paper would mock her until she felt like she was bleeding. Only then would words appear. She'd begin with one word, and by the time she'd have finished a page, the sky would be dark. By 9pm, she'd collapse into a fitful sleep and awake to her brother rocketing around the living room at 5am.

It was during revision some nights that he would appear, a tupperware container of popcorn for them both to share. She'd follow him and sit down on the sofa, a countdown ticking inside her head. Harry gripped her hand when they watched the show together. Her fingers disappeared inside his fist. Wrist throbbing, she'd watch his eyes bob up and down like fish in a tank. He would cheer when necessary and boo when not and yelled the characters names as they appeared on screen. His voice reminded her of Scooby Doo, a drawl with lisped w's and sharp g's.

Sometimes, she found herself mouthing the dialogue. When she felt her lips moving, she'd bite her cheek until it bled, and the foamy liquid halted her incantation.

Schooldays existed as a holiday to normalcy. That temporary world held political movements, algebraic equations and eloquent sonnets. And then, in the evening, she was home again. The moment she crossed the threshold of the front door, the verbal fog would descend. Her inner voice ceased to exist, replaced by the thumping of his footsteps or the relentless singing of the Thomas theme tune. Outside her room, he'd pace like an elephant trapped in a cage. Backwards and forwards, his voice rising and falling as he bounded by her door. Some nights, she imagined him tripping, his head bashing against the wooden floor, air crackling with his cry. In others, she saw images of him in different lives – a bank robber plundering loot, an Olympic athlete aiming for gold.

Dinners were the hardest. They were signalled by a reprieve from cartoon dialogue, followed by a shout from the kitchen. Danielle would finish the homework problem she was on as methodically as possible, writing every alternative answer in flourishing detail. Her inner voice rumbled with delight, able to be heard. Then a knock, only once, and she'd rise like a marionette.

The amount of new noise always startled her. Scraping forks, tongues smacking, fingertips drumming on mahogany wood. Her arms felt encased in clay, and so she ate slowly. Each mouthful was punished by the glimmer of what lay underneath. Mashed potato revealed a black eyeball. Steamed broccoli uncovered the rungs of the train track. Gravy discoloured the font and muddied the colours. The trains soon revealed themselves, grinning with mirth. And each night, she vowed to fracture their smiles with a slam across the countertop. She never did.

'Harry loves when we all use these plates,' her mother had

said once, fingers flying over the keyboard.

'Please do it. For him. You can read my blog post about it if you want?'

She had. The post was long and whimsical – a creation myth of his trials and tribulations. 'But look at how far he had come', she always ended with. How much he loved it when the family ate off his Thomas plates.

Commenters in the thousands would point out their humility and strength, buzzwords to make 'special families' feel better about their situation. 'Inspirational' was another one thrown out with little subjectivity.

Harry existed, and that was enough to earn merit.

On the weekends, when Harry's snores would creep out from under his door, she'd sneak into the kitchen and unpack their other plates. They were her grandmother's, swamp green, worn from repeated use. A thin crack ran along their underside. She'd stare at them in the dim flicker of the kitchen light. It reminded her of religious persecution – a small shrine of her outlawed faith hidden underneath their kitchen sink.

The selection of the plate was one of the very few rituals that involved her. He'd brandish the chosen plate like a gun five minutes before mealtime. Outside her door, he stared with arrowed eyes and plate cocked.

He'd present it to her for inspection, but not let her take it in her hands. Three seconds was the optimum time to examine it. Any longer and he'd snort and stamp his foot. 'I like it,' she would say, and he would bound away for another few moments of peace.

The other was worse. At 8:30pm, he'd wrap her in his shaggy arms and press his lips against her own. 'Night night,' he said, his mouth thick with saliva. She never hugged him back.

Her second cousin coughed.

'I'm sorry, I shouldn't have brought it up.'

Danielle looked at him and the sheepish way he hung his head. She smiled with her teeth. 'They're going as well as they can be.'

She fingered the cigarette from its packet and lit up underneath the solitary oak. From the window, she could still see people bumbling around inside. She blew smoke towards them, masking the red and green flashes of their costumes.

Smoking wasn't something she enjoyed, but it made her feel adult. And Harry hated it. She wondered if her parents cared, but apart from a tired scolding, they had done nothing to stop her.

She flicked the ash into the grass. Harry had stopped hugging her towards the end, complaining that she smelt of smoke. She'd hang her head out the window and light one up, sucking the nicotine as quickly as possible. The smell clung to her hair, but not her room. He'd come in and leave as quickly as he arrived, and she'd smile so wide her jaw hurt.

The funeral director stepped out from the hall and strode over until he was under the tree.

'Do you mind?' He said.

She looked him up and down, in a costume she had seen hundreds of times on TV. It suited him, and she felt tension drain from her shoulders.

'No. Feel free.'

They smoked in silence for a while. People had begun to leave – cousins and aunts and uncles who would shed their costumes in wardrobes or donate them to charity shops. They all waved to her, and she raised her hand. 'All aboard!' Harry would have yelled. She said nothing.

She finished, and as she ground the butt with her heel, she

said, 'I bet this is the weirdest funeral you've been to.'

The director took a deep drag, the exhale of smoke floating up towards the bony tendrils of the branches. He looked towards the sky and said, 'It's the most unique, yes.' He paused, and then said, 'But it's also one of the nicest. You can tell he was really loved.'

Danielle crushed her inner cheek between her teeth until it filled with blood. She lapped at it with her tongue as she walked away.

The car ride home was rhythmic. The clicking of the indicator, her mother's steam train nails clanking against her phone. The shops and restaurants blurred past. Most, she realised, she had never been in.

Five minutes from their home, the train station filled her view. A train had halted, the commuters shifting off towards their next destination. She imagined Harry standing among them, a train guard answering questions, or a driver taking a break. His last visit to a station had resulted in covered ears and erratic howls, heightened with each screech of the train's brakes. It had made her cry too.

And then they were home. Danielle was the first inside. She heard her mother's call about dinner and did not respond. Plates were already laid out at the table. Their eyes followed her, indignant at being ignored.

His bedroom door was shut, and she could hear her own footsteps pound towards her room. Her bed lay splayed with coursework, neon markers and worn-down pencil shavings sleeping on her pillow. She shut her door with an audible click.

She had not cried since his death. She had squeezed her eyes shut and pinched herself and yelled wordlessly into the bathroom mirror. But she couldn't. The Thomas the Tank

Engine jingle rattled inside her brain. She realised the loop was infinite, and it only grew softer or louder with the thump of her heart.

Danielle found herself mouthing the words again. She hunched her back, buried her face in the duvet and thumbed at the pin inside her pocket. Off in the distance, a train whistled a shriek into the night. She imagined being on that train. Slipping onto one of the seats, ticket burning a hole in her pocket. She would roll off into the night, the remnants of her town shifting into blurred bricks and signposts. When she'd open her eyes, they would have arrived in a desolate spot of countryside. The wind would overpower every noise, and she'd wander through the blades of grass and up the hills and fill her head with nature's songs.

But even then, she knew she'd still hear him, crisp and clear, asking if she wanted to watch Thomas. And she knew, even though he wasn't real anymore, that she would say yes.

Outtakes From Teenage Cantos

Kit Ingram

One

Darkness thickens in the hourglass as I drive downward.
   Lights of red giants or the brakes of lorries, maybe.
Warm air streaks through the vent, damp with
   the smell of green hay and barn animals.
I blink through the bug splatter, a filter for
   the moonglow as it crawls across the windscreen.
(Big surprise when your life is smeared out of existence.)
   I turn down the musings of pop angels and
listen to the steady *hee-oosh* of Jack's breathing.
   The constellations, if they're out there, are
     dreaming up better stories for themselves.

Two

Fuel meter says *Keep going, kid*, so I skip over the lake of fire.
   I have a moment where I see the Olsens kneeling in
some Mormon temple, a shaft of light plucking the tuned
   strings of their souls. No morning coffee, no blood of
Christ, just that godly beam firing their happy
   hormones into overdrive. The Littlest Olsen used to
play with my brother and me, mostly a game where we
   battled with Wild West figurines from the pound
store.
I can't remember the name of my tribe, the one
   blown into a rubble of tomahawks, anyway.
The Olsens must have got a real kick out of us,
    the depth of our meekness.

Three

I won't tell you I've contemplated murder,
  but right now, I can see it flashing in the distance,
a tin rocket, hot as Hell. Every face of a kid who whispered
  under their breath, thinking I wouldn't hear,
hisses by like a tongue of brimstone.
  I'm not a violent person, never played those shoot 'em
games that went viral, but I have a good imagination.
  The visions are wreathed in a silvery light, gauzy
apparitions of kids snuff out like whispers and rise
  out of their horror suits to float among stars.

The Stuffed Minimalist

Roan Ellis-O'Neill

Highly Commended

As avenues line up with trees,
and drones drop seeds in Myanmar
and Greta Thunberg sails the Atlantic Ocean with Australian
    YouTube influencers
and your man carries a coffee flask the size of his head
        and I won't ask him about his worryingly high intake
    of caffeinated products
and Bowie warns me that we only have five years left,
I wonder if we could send the Liberal Democrats to Dignitas.

As the tortoise yearns for the hare's loving care
    and the sophomore preceptor whips the students
    into a shape that stymies curiosity,
        repeats "who are *they*? Don't look at your book.
    Who are *they*?"
and Galaxie 500 collaborate, not cover, New Order's
    "Ceremony" in my headphones
and the staff member for whom I turn on the microphones
asks me why I've had a bad
        experience here then yaps on about how
        terrorist attacks in Germany
        prevent him from emigrating there,
and he attempts to find common ground in snow-fluttering
    existence,
        raking my mind across the patio doors where he
        dreams the dream of peace and harmony where
        terrorists die off stage
and the DVD collection stagnates into a passive archive

because nobody watches DVDs anymore
and they only seem to gather dust,
I question why don't they just inject the carbon back
into the rocks.

As the Queen abolishes Coronation chicken sandwiches
and *British Vogue* ask two-hundred-and-seventy-eight
questions to Iggy Pop regarding his
chameleon and choice of brie
and dried cranberries simmer in sauces quadrupling the
high-oleic sunflower oil percentage
among the red-stained paper prompts
and we pour our passions down the esophagus where the
train has arrived
thirty-two minutes late up the smokestack of my
menthol cigarette,
I buy a suitcase and close my inventory.

Mixology

Sue Finlay

(Extracts from: A Guide to Life's Cocktails)

Dad's Fruit Punch@The Willows, Alconberry Weston
If you are drinking Dad's Fruit Punch, make sure that no one at the party sees you. It will be in a huge, silver-plated tureen with six lion heads embossed around the side. The colour of the punch won't match any of the colouring pencils in your Bumper 100 Crayola Set and your big brother, Steve, will have told you that it smells like Mr Brady's chemistry lab. There will be pieces of apple and slices of orange sloshing around in it. Dad will be using a silver ladle to serve it into cut glass tumblers and handing it out to the guests as they arrive. Mum will be wearing a sparkly trouser suit and will be wandering round the guests with a plate of vol-au-vents. You will be in red ladybird pyjamas from Woolworths. Briefly wonder if Steve has noticed his favourite Scooby Doo pencil topper is missing as you squeeze it in your pocket.

When Dad leaves the fruit punch station to talk to Phil from Business Studies, sidle over and pretend to stir it, but ladle some into Steve's Scooby Doo mug. When you look up, Varsha from Legal will be watching you, but she'll wink. Decide to be like Varsha when you grow up. Put a couple of sausage rolls and cocktail stick skewers in your pocket and make for the stairs, where Steve will be waiting. Take a quick slug from the Scooby Doo mug before you hand it over to him. While you are coughing, he will have downed it in a oner. He'll stand up and beat his chest with his fists and say 'scooby dooby doo' in a silly voice that makes you laugh.

Sit on the stairs and eat the sausage rolls and cocktail stick skewers. When you have finished, Steve will stand up and try to fart in your face and you will scream. He'll put you in a headlock. Stab him in the leg with the cocktail stick.

Brandy and Babycham@Student Union bar, Freshers Week
If you have ordered Brandy and Babycham, make sure it's your fifth one before loudly exclaiming that alcohol doesn't really affect you that much and you can drink literally gallons before feeling anything. Laugh like a hyena at Benji's joke about his parents dropping him off and his mum crying. When Golden Brown comes on the jukebox, pretend to know all the lyrics and tell everyone you've seen The Stranglers live *at least* ten times.

Drink three more Brandy and Babychams before falling into the arms of Reagan, who will drag you off to the loos. While you are being sick, listen to her telling you she fancies Mike. Don't tell her you fancy him too. Never tell her. Stagger back to the bar arm in arm and announce that there's a party round your place tonight. Crowd into the off-licence at the end of your road, then pile into the Chippie next door for bags of steaming hot chips. Burn the roof of your mouth off eating them too quickly.

Watch Benji run up the middle of the road towards you wearing a traffic cone on his head, his arms outstretched. Feel alive. Feel free.

Bellinis@The Big Party Barn, Cotswolds
If you are drinking Bellinis at Reagan's Hen Party Weekend, you will be using penis straws to drink them. You will be sitting in a hot tub wearing pink fluffy Deely boppers that say 'head bridesmaid'. Also in the hot tub will be Phoebe, Emily and Chloe from uni, Esther, Becka, Ruby and Ems from home, Reagan's mum, and someone called Pam.

After a while, no one will bother making Bellinis, they'll just pour prosecco straight into random tumblers they've found in the cupboards. Pam won't even bother with the tumbler. Later on, when it gets to playing Mr and Mrs, Reagan's mum will take over. She'll have been emailing Mike questions for the past two weeks. Laugh with everyone else when Reagan gets an answer wrong, even though you know the right answer.

Slip outside for some fresh air. Walk to the end of the garden. Pam will be there smoking, and she'll offer you a cigarette. Take it. Inhale deeply and hold the smoke in your lungs before letting it drift lazily out of your mouth. Don't think about any of it, just let the nicotine do its work.

Sex on the Beach@All-inclusive, Jamaica

If you have ordered Sex on the Beach, make sure you drink it in the Caribbean, sitting on a stool at a bar that has a fringe of dried palms. There will be a coating of sand on your ankles, like sugar on shortbread.

When the bartender places the cocktail in front of you, don't ask him if he used premium spirits to make it. He will have a white gash of a smile that cuts through his tan and eyes that read you like a high-end magazine, flicking through, casually.

Part your salt-dried lips, place them around the straw, then turn away. Don't think about your divorce or what your mum said. Draw deeply. Put on your aviators. Let your sarong drift down from your right shoulder. Wave to Mike and Reagan as they walk hand in hand along the shoreline. Try not to swallow, just let it slide down your throat. Enjoy the coldness then the warmth as it enters your brain. Sigh.

When you get to the end, don't suck the dregs, leave them. Turn back to the bartender. He will be leaning at the other end of the bar, waiting. You won't have to say a thing.

Raspberry Crush@The Vicarage, St Nicholas Parish Church
If you are drinking a Raspberry Crush, it will be because you are standing in the garden of the Vicarage after the christening of Zephie Aura.

You will be making polite conversation with the vicar. Zephie will be sleeping blissfully in your arms, having screamed blue murder in the church only ten minutes ago. She will be wearing white socks and a floral print dress edged with lace. One of the socks will be dangling, half off, waiting to fall. The vicar will be enquiring politely about your religious qualifications to be a godmother. Deflect by smiling and lying about all the charities you support. When you look up, Mike will be watching you. Look away.

Reagan will come up from behind and encircle you and Zephie in her arms. She will very subtly whisper something naughty about the vicar while pretending to tuck your hair behind your ear. Clamp your lips tight shut so as not to laugh. You will hear a distant hum of insects as they buzz around the buffet.

Zephie will stir dreamily in your arms, her lips making a tiny 'o' shape. Stroke her cheek with your finger. Mike will walk across the lawn and take her from you, gently, without waking her, and kiss her forehead. Feel lost. Feel alone.

Gin and Tonic@The Ivy, West Street, London
If you are drinking a Gin and Tonic at The Ivy, the bartender will ask you what gin you want. He will hand you a menu and wait. Turn the pages as though you know what you are looking for, then point at one. He will nod sagely and spend a long time on it. He will present it to you in an overlarge glass bowl on a long stem, with ribbons of shaved cucumber and two or three black peppercorns floating around the surface.

Take it to a corner table where you can watch people. Try to ignore the middle-aged lady sitting on her own. She will be waving her arms around and talking about how no one knows how to make a proper gin and tonic these days. She might be talking to you, but you can't be sure. Nod, but don't meet her eye.

Look at your phone and check that this was the right venue and the right time. Sip slowly. Don't be tipsy, just relaxed. When Arlo enters, check your phone to see if his photo matches his profile picture. Watch him closely as he goes to the bar and orders a drink. Don't introduce yourself until you have decided if he is okay or not. Decide what okay means at this point in your life. When you are satisfied that he is acceptable, leave the table and go over. He will be quietly spoken, attentive, and he will make you laugh. Allow yourself to be charmed. When he asks if you'd like another drink, don't hesitate. Say yes.

Warm oat milk with a dash of whisky@St Luke's Hospice
If you are drinking warm oat milk, make sure you take a hip flask of whisky to add to it, hidden in your handbag. Before you enter the building, steel yourself. Mike and Zephie will be in the cafe downstairs and will leap up when they see you. You will all hug and try not to cry. They will fill you in on how things are. You will go up to Reagan's room and walk up and down for ten minutes, taking deep breaths, before you go in.

Reagan will do her best attempt at a smile. There will be oxygen tubes sticking out of her nose and a canister sitting at her side. The suck and draw will be a musical backdrop as you sit on her bed. Make her laugh by likening the sound to the sucking of Bellinis through a penis straw. Lay your head in her lap. She will stroke your hair. Tell her you love her. Tell her what she means to you. Don't cry. She will say that she is sorry about Mike, that she knew all along how you felt. Say no. Say it doesn't matter.

When the nurse comes in with warmed oat milk, wait for

her to leave before taking the hip flask out of your bag. Slosh it in. Hold the cup to her mouth and let her take a sip, before taking a slug yourself from the same cup. She will try to make a joke about it tasting like Brandy and Babycham, before falling asleep. Tiptoe out. Shut the door quietly so as not to wake her.

Champagne and canapes@Edinburgh University
If you are drinking Champagne and eating canopes, make sure you are standing in a white marquee in the grounds of the McEwan Hall. The sides of the marquee will be flapping about, angrily. You will be wearing a summer dress but wishing you hadn't.

Zephie will be wearing a black gown and mortar board. She will be high, ecstatic, joyous. Her friends will be the same. They will be laughing and hugging and taking group pictures and selfies. There will be no end to their delight. Parents and family will be cradling drinks and stuffing canopes into their mouths, watching on. Zephie will throw her arms around you and thank you for coming. She will drag you off to meet Lissie, Ava, Isabel, Calum and Luke. They will say 'Hi' and talk politely to you for a few minutes. Move away. Let them get on with it.

Stand next to Mike and chink glasses. Don't say you must be so proud. Wait for him to speak.

Look at his grey hair and his slight stoop. He will produce a black and white photograph of your graduation. Fish your reading glasses out of your bag. Look at it and say, 'look at us'. He will ask if you remember that night, after Reagan had gone to bed. Take the photograph from him and stare at Reagan. She will be smiling directly at the camera, jubilant, happy. You and Mike will be turned towards her. Say gosh what a long time ago.

After you hand the photograph back, tell him you must go,

you have a plane to catch. Hug him tightly. Feel his skin on your skin. Smell his aftershave. Wave goodbye to Zephie. Walk away.

All in the Meaning

Alison Nuorto

In memory of an ex, who took his own life in 2019

Had I known that I would never see you again,
I would have memorized every line and arc of your frame
And giddily inhaled your scent, that I cannot recall.
I would have milked the textures from the mundane,
Wrung every minute dry,
Gorged on every syllable
And clawed out every thought,
To recreate you in the hollow night
And inflate you into the void between my sheets;
Where... I would cling to you.

Hecuba

Kenneth Hickey

Men's lawless lusts are all called love

She sits alone in the cool grey dawn
At the fractured make-up mirror
Hiding the work of his heavy hand
In the silence of sleeping children's dreams.

The cyclops breathes heavily on the bed
Devourer of sweetest human flesh
Guarding all approaches to this high tower
No helmeted knight rides from Camelot.

She whispers low to the virgin mother
Only fragile panting prayers remain
In time there will be flowers; muted apologies
The earth rights on its axis again.

Till savage beast unmasks once more
Beating bright beauty to the unwashed floor.

She fixes her smile; continues to weep
And waits for the man to die in his sleep.

The Man Who Loves Tchaikovsky Beats his Wife: A Symphony in Four Movements

Sara Keating

Highly Commended

1. Op. 39. Album Pour Enfants (1878)

Once upon a time, I shared a bed with my mother. She had straight black hair as long as Rapunzel's. One night, The Man Who Loves Tchaikovsky pulled her from the bed by her plait as I held onto her nightdress. My sister in the cot by the wall was crying.

Once upon a time, my mother fell down the stairs in the middle of the night. The Man Who Loves Tchaikovsky said she tripped over a toy I had left in the upstairs hallway. My mother has a shiny pink scar that runs wrist to elbow on her forearm, like a zip sewn shut.

Once upon a time, we were driving into town, my mother in the front seat beside The Man Who Loves Tchaikovsky. The car was still moving when he stretched across her and opened the door and pushed her onto the road. My sister and I didn't say anything as The Man Who Loves Tchaikovsky parked the car and took us in to see his favourite painting in the gallery.

Once upon a time, the police came to the door when The Man Who Loves Tchaikovsky was in a red, red mood. He took them to his study, where the piano was. I could not hear through the door which voice was his. They all sounded like The Man Who Loves Tchaikovsky, or maybe none of them did.

Once upon a time, my mother asked me if she should leave The Man Who Loves Tchaikovsky, and I said yes, yes, yes, and briefly imagined a future without him. I was twelve years old, and she could not.

2. Op. 42. Souvenir d'un Lieu Cher (1878)

Everybody loves The Man Who Loves Tchaikovsky. He can play The Twelve Seasons on the piano without sheet music, and he hosts parties themed around the ballets in winter. Once, he bought tutus for my sister and I and stood us on upturned tea crates in the corner. We turned slowly like plastic figures in a music box all night, dancing with our arms.

The Man Who Loves Tchaikovsky has a silver tongue. People lean in to hear him proclaim the end of art/ambition/the civilised world, and they believe him.

The Man Who Loves Tchaikovsky has lots of friends. He goes out early in the morning to have breakfast in their hotel rooms, stays out late drinking whiskey in their mansions. He cannot bear the sight of us, he says when he returns, the squalor.

The house does not feel like home when The Man Who Loves Tchaikovsky is not there to fill it with his music. My sister and I sit all day at the window in our bedroom overlooking the driveway, waiting for him to come back, the noise to begin.

The Man Who Loves Tchaikovsky loves Tchaikovsky more than any of us. When my mother asks my sister and I about our day in school at the dinner table, he stands up and turns the music on the radio up as loud as it will go.

The Man Who Loves Tchaikovsky has two faces, like the statue in the entrance to the museum he brings us to on Sundays. The stone profiles are almost identical. My sister and I cannot pinpoint exactly what makes the one that faces the door so expansive and kind, and the one that faces into the room so mean and ugly.

3. Op. 47. Dusk Fell on the Earth (1880)

The Man Who Loves Tchaikovsky doesn't always love Tchaikovsky. Sometimes, he takes the records from their sleeves and breaks them in two. Sometimes, the police bring him home, and he doesn't use his nice voice when he is talking to them, or when he is talking to my mother in front of them. Sometimes, he leaves with them again and doesn't come back for days.

Even Tchaikovsky hated his wife, The Man Who Loves Tchaikovsky says. She was so disgusting, he slept with men and killed himself. The Man Who Loves Tchaikovsky says that everybody knows great men must make their wives suffer. It is a necessary sacrifice.

The Man Who Loves Tchaikovsky's friends stop answering the door when he calls in the evenings, tell the porter not to let him in.

The Man Who Loves Tchaikovsky's hands tremble now when

he plays the piano. Warming up with a scherzo one night, The Man Who Loves Tchaikovsky fumbles the scales and hits the keys so hard he breaks a string. He takes a sledgehammer to the piano and carries it out to the garden, piece by piece.

The Man Who Loves Tchaikovsky wears his tweed suit every day, though he has nowhere to go to. My mother scrubs the vomit from his shirt in the morning before applying her makeup, powdering The Man Who Loves Tchaikovsky's fingerprints away.

The police find The Man Who Loves Tchaikovsky on the pier, on the railway bridge, in the laneway between the concert hall and the gallery. When they bring him home, my mother puts him to bed like a child.

4. Op. 52. All Night Vigil (1882)

The Man Who Loves Tchaikovsky is spotted in the local Tesco in his pyjamas putting cans of cider and bottles of champagne into a trolley. Someone calls my mother, who calls me down from the bedroom and asks me to go with her to find him.

The next morning, when Tchaikovsky comes on the radio, The Man Who Loves Tchaikovsky beats my mother around the head with the metronome and cuts his wrists with a kitchen knife.

When the ambulance comes to get her, the paramedics take The Man Who Loves Tchaikovsky away as well.

The Man Who Loves Tchaikovsky looks small in the hospital bed without his glasses. His silk dressing gown is hanging on the back of the door. From the nurse's station, the trumpets and horns are moaning, plaintive, in Tchaikovsky's Symphony No 6: Pathetique.

My mother sits beside The Man Who Loves Tchaikovsky keeping vigil, humming Tchaikovsky's Wedding March through broken teeth. Once upon a time, they used to polka back and forth across his study, my sister lifting and replacing the needle every time the mazurka frenzied to a stop.

This is, after all, The Man Who Loves Tchaikovsky.

Daddy

Anna Seidel

means to feel suffocated under diving bells,
to whisper secrets into marble carved auricles,
to be grazed by bullets of misfired words,
unheard prayers pouring into pillows,
looking up into a sky of bruised cloud-castles,
the fear of something overlooked,
the loneliness felt by the unlanguaged,
compulsively rearranging plot twists from scant facts.
But I remain powerless to change the picture,
starved for warm words, for hugging laughter.
A destitute criminal, I dream of thieving parts of
"dad" and "da-da" for the silly girl inside
that waits and waits.
Febrile and with the alertness of a burglar,
I enter the room, alive with your breathing.
The moon magically streaming, breaks its sheaf of colors
on the chattering teeth of window blinds,
rays of light reflections spritzing crimson tails
on strewn pages of your manuscript.
I eat paper one by one, the scripted bodies
attended to with benevolent passion.
Maybe you worried for too many souls to see mine.
And I chew on bittersweet ink juice dripping
from the curled-up cellulose balls reminding
of forbidden fruit. And I'd imagine
how you'd wake to scream "no" and "don't",
and speaking without words, that silly girl breathes
into the cavity of your skull
what it means to feel pain paralyzed.

Survivor

Tiffany Carrington

Flowers sit on the kitchen table that he sent,
Another apology from last night's argument.
It's not his fault, it's really mine,
I should know not to step out of line.
I shouldn't have gone out last night with friends,
He just wanted to spend time with me at the weekend.
So what if he doesn't allow me to be free,
At least he doesn't hit me.

A necklace sparkles in a cushioned box,
Shows that he must love me a lot.
He is sorry, that much is obvious,
I can understand why he was so jealous.
I shouldn't have worn that dress last night,
It showed off too much skin, and it wasn't right.
He didn't like the way the waiter looked at me with lust,
It wouldn't have happened if I had only covered up.
I guess it's okay if he's more jealous than I would like him to
be,
At least he doesn't hit me.

As I look at the new ring shimmering on my finger,
The hurt from his poisoned words still lingers.
This morning I made his coffee wrong,
He got mad and threw it on the floor.
He says it's my fault for not making it right,
It's always my fault every time we fight.
But I don't deserve to be treated this way,
So, I pack my bags whilst he's away.
I don't want it, if this is what they call love,

I have to leave, I've enough.
As I walk out the door, I can't help but feel guilty
Afterall, at least he didn't hit me.

His punches never touched my face,
His punches hit me in a different place.
The scars he left behind are not on my skin,
The pain goes much deeper within.
It's hard to get away from someone, when they're all you
know.
How do you pick yourself up, when you feel so low?
It isn't as easy as they think it is,
When I've been captured by his kiss.
But I will not make that same excuse,
He didn't hit me, but it was still abuse.

Caramel

Lucy Pearce

It's been a while,
The cogs stuck still

Hair and flesh wound around the engine pieces,
slipped between the metal
and stopped

Homes filled with thick fog and damp carpets,
every limb slow as we swam through caramel,
spoke through a tube

We hold hands and cry over our coffees,
let them grow cold and old
until the milk starts to lump

We link arms and weep around the TV,
let the screen switch to standby
and watch the red burn in

We rub shoulders and sob in public gardens,
collecting glances and hushed voices
that drip freely from our backs

Abiding sadness floats upon stagnant weeks,
embroidering delicate flesh like ink coloured poison

Abiding sadness sits, uninvited, in our kitchen,
sipping tea we never made it,
eating food we never cooked it

Hair and flesh wound around the engine pieces,
slipped between the metal
and stopped

So we stopped,
and started swimming through caramel.

Pieces of Her Child

Chris Edwards-Pritchard

Margot drew the curtains and loaded a spool of white filament into the machine on Robert's desk. She hit print on a file titled: 'Rob_head_1'. The machine whirred, and slim panels of light at the back and sides pulsed to life, illuminating her face in a gentle way, like an artefact at the Natural History Museum.

Exhibit A: 51-year-old Margot Higgs poking around in her son's empty bedroom at 2am. The file was a three-dimensional scan of her son, taken earlier that summer on the morning of his farewell family barbeque. Robert wore shorts, a nice shirt, and flip-flops, and stood perfectly still in the centre of the living room, which Margot had decked out with balloons and banners and a fold-out table of crisps, olives and micro-quiches, all clingfilmed. Chairs from the attic filled up the room's usual gaps and spaces. Margot wore a fancy magnolia dress and her hair had been styled at the salon in the centre of town for the first time in years. She held the iPad out in front of her to take the scan of her son, shuffling slowly around the room, then standing on a chair to capture his curls from above. On the screen, his model took shape; at first fibrous scaffolding, then distinct features like thin lips and the same jawline that once belonged to his father, Glen, before Glen ate all of those pies.

It was nice.

It was a nice moment.

It's not every day you get to just look at your grown-up child like that.

Margot smiled into the light of the machine.

The print bed rose up to meet the extruder nozzle, and the extruder nozzle roamed in not-quite-perfect ovals to deposit the first few layers of Robert's neck, jerking every now and then to account for moles and veins and the pointed V of his Adam's apple. The plastic smelled funny and familiar, like gas and air, which had a medical name that Glen would probably know. He had become a general knowledge whore since Robert left home, cramming himself full of capital cities and presidents and prime numbers. It gave them something to do in the evenings. Margot asked questions from a quizzing app and Glen answered them. Every time he got one wrong, she celebrated a small, quiet victory.

Margot sat there in the dark, watching Robert's neck build into Robert's jawline, and Robert's jawline build into Robert's petal thin lips. It was one in the afternoon in Sydney, and Actual Robert would be starting his shift soon; he had only been gone for three weeks and had already taken a job on the checkouts. Margot sent him a message on WhatsApp and added the dancing lady emoji, the fierce dancer in a red dress. Her favourite. The woman she wanted to be. The print had five hours remaining, so Margot left it running and carefully closed the door, and when she turned to walk along the landing, there was Glen, peering out of the darkness of their bedroom in a drooping vest and the world's biggest boxer shorts.

'Sleeping in there again?' he said.

'No, just couldn't nod off.'

'Well, it's not exactly hushabye mountain in here.'

'Sorry?' said Margot.

'Next door,' he said. 'They're at it again.'

Glen pointed at the wall behind their bed and disappeared into the bathroom for a piss. Ah, yes. Their new next door neighbours, Keith and Julie, both in their late fifties, were having sex again. There she goes, with the *yeses* and the *oh God oh God oh Gods*. Julie accounted for 99% of the noise and occasionally there were other sounds – smacking, maybe whipping – but not tonight. Margot knew very little about these people living on the other side of the wall; sometimes, she took in their Amazon parcels when they weren't around. Keith would knock on the door in the evening with his grey beard and long gunmetal hair all slicked back, and the act of touching the boxes and passing the boxes into his arms made her feel somehow part of it all, somehow implicit in their constant coitus. How did they do it? That's what Margot wanted to know. How did they keep it up? Literally, in Keith's case. She grabbed an empty glass from the bedside table and held it against the wall to get a closer listen.

The next morning, Margot found Glen in the kitchen cutting the rind off rashers of bacon, which was his idea of healthy eating. The microwave hummed and there were sausages and hash browns in the oven. Glen and Robert had been getting up early on Tuesdays to have a fry up and watch the new episode of *Spectrum* before any spoilers surfaced on social media or at work. It was just about the only time they spent together. Glen called it quality father-and-son time, whereas Robert only watched the show with his father in the first place because Margot told him it would be a nice idea whilst Glen was out of work and on antidepressants. This was ten years ago. Little did Robert know that *Spectrum* would run for seven seasons and counting.

    'Do you know if Rob watched it?' asked Margot.

    'You tell me,' said Glen.

    Glen had this thing about Robert only ever messaging Margot. He scooped up the trimmings of bacon fat and dropped them in the bin. Not the food bin, but whatever. Margot sat at the breakfast bar and scrolled through Instagram.

    'How was the show, then?' she said. Which is what she always used to ask the two of them on a Tuesday morning.

'Caleb died,' said Glen. 'Tyson chopped his head off and stored it in the fridge.' That sounded like something of a tone-change for *Spectrum*, but Glen seemed pretty happy about it, so maybe it was a mid-season alternate future filler jobbie. Glen smiled whilst laying down rashers of bacon on a frying pan, like a Vegas croupier.

'Really? Didn't he just get engaged?'

'Could you grab the butter?' said Glen.

'Oh,' said Margot. 'Sure.'

Margot continued scrolling as she took out the butter and handed it to Glen.

'What's the name for gas and air?' she asked.

'What?'

'You know, gas and air, in hospitals.'

Glen looked at her.

Next to him the bacon sizzled, and tiny droplets of oil spat overboard like hailstones.

'Did you even look in the fridge?' he said.

Margot gestured towards the tub of butter.

'You did say butter, right?' she said.

'Yes.'

'So?'

'So, how did you miss it?' said Glen.

Margot crunched her eyebrows. Glen downed his spatula and opened the fridge like a gameshow host to reveal Robert's now fully printed plastic head wedged in between the tomatoes and a ready-meal lasagne. Bright and white, with a long anchor nose and kind eyes, and the two front teeth pushing together in a way that braces were never able to remedy. Teeth from her side of the family. Margot went cold and felt her body drain; for a second, the decapitation was real and vivid, and then she remembered the machine in the middle of the night.

'What the hell?' said Margot, taking the head out of the

fridge.

Plum tomatoes came tumbling out, but she didn't care.

Glen laughed. He laughed as if there were other people in the room.

'Oh come on,' he said.

'Why would you do this? This is not funny.'

'It's a little bit funny.'

'It's our son's head for Christ's sake.'

Glen closed the fridge and kept his hand tight on the handle.

'It's just a prank, Margot.'

'Since when do we do pranks?' she said.

Glen's knuckles were white like larvae.

'Why the hell have you printed his head in the first place?'

'Robert showed me how to use the printer,' she said. 'I actually pay attention to his interests.'

'Well, he can't be that interested if he left the damn thing behind.'

'Your bacon is burning,' said Margot.

Margot walked out the room with the cold plastic head tucked between her hip and her arm.

Glen left the house at eight o'clock that morning. Margot called in sick to the local primary where she worked as a chef three days a week (a job she started when Robert first went to school all those years ago), then took Robert's head upstairs and placed it on the rug in the middle of their bedroom, where she used to sit him as a baby, and climbed into bed. She heard a noise coming from the back wall. It was Julie.

Oh yes ohhh yes, said Julie. Margot sat up and groped around for the TV remote, but she couldn't find it. She looked at Robert's head and Robert's head looked at her, then she slipped under the duvet and held the fabric tight around her face, like vacuum-packed steak but, if anything, it was worse.

She could even feel the vibrations, *yes*, as late-fifties Julie bounced up and down on late-fifties Keith. As the movement pulsed through to Margot, she thought about it, then thought better of it, then let her hand slide down her stomach and then, yes, why not, why the hell not. Except, no. Not with Robert in the same room.

That had always been her reason: not with Robert in the house. In the top drawer of Glen's bedside table, underneath the passports and marriage certificate, there was a box of condoms that had expired seven years ago. Margot pulled herself out of bed and took a shower.

For years, Margot had a suitcase of clothes and some money stashed at the back of the cupboard on her side of the bed. Glen came across the suitcase one day whilst trying to find a hiding place for Robert's fifth birthday present.

'It doesn't mean anything,' said Margot. 'It's just symbolic.'

'Symbolic?' said Glen. 'What does that even mean?'

She didn't really know.

Glen was not a bad guy. He did okay, all things considered. He made it all the way through to his late twenties being this funny and caring guy who worked out and went down on his wife, and sure he had the occasional tantrum and the occasional slump, no more than the rest of us, but then he got caught in the gravitational pull of a well-paid job and found himself managing a team of people; then firing some of them, then missing Robert's bathtime because of a 'crisis' ('Oh you want a crisis? How about the baby shitting all over the sofa?'), then taking phone calls with clients late into the evening and telling Margot it was his friend Gary on the phone, (because she was worried he had no friends) when he hadn't spoken to Gary in years.

That was just the beginning. Work sucked him in and churned him up. Responsibility tightened all around him like a boa. The more he worked, the less he saw Margot and Robert, and the less he saw Margot and Robert, the less he felt like he really belonged at home. At forty-three, Glen was made redundant from the bank in a 'digital transformation' restructure. He got hammered and lost his wallet and pissed himself on the District Line. Then he made a call to the home phone to explain to Margot that he'd been drugged by one of his colleagues, and how it would just be better for everyone if he ceased to exist. They had decent life insurance, after all. But Margot wasn't there, and fifteen-year-old Robert answered the phone instead.

Margot had her shower and got dressed. She picked up Robert's head and came downstairs. In the kitchen, she noticed a post-it note on the counter which said: entonox. She took out her phone to googled entonox and found that it was the medical name for gas and air. Margot placed Robert's head next to the note and ate her lunch on the sofa in front of the extended edition of *The Return of the King*, which was her and Robert's joint favourite film. Or perhaps he had a new favourite now? They saw it at the cinema five times in the winter of 2003. Glen offered to take Robert on his own, but Robert said that he only wanted to go with Margot. The doorbell rang halfway through the Mouth of Sauron scene, so Margot paused the TV. Frankie and her five-year-old daughter Gracie were at the front door. They lived on the other side of Margot and Glen.

'Thank God you're in,' said Frankie.

'What's the matter?' said Margot, and then 'hello lovely' to Gracie, who was busy twirling on one leg.

'Would you mind watching her for an hour?'

'An hour?'

'Two maximum.'

Margot smiled.

Gracie ran through to the living room and Frankie mouthed *thank you.*

'Is everything okay?' said Margot.

'Emergency board meeting. I thought you were at work yourself?'

'Called in sick this morning.'

'Oh, Margot you should have said, don't worry I'll find someone else.'

'It's fine, I'm fine, I'm–'

'What's this?' said Gracie.

Gracie ran towards them holding up Robert's plastic head in her tiny hands. Margot laughed and said it was a craft project and told Gracie to get the pens out of the activity box in the dining room. Gracie nodded and scrunched her cheeks up into a smile.

At four o'clock, Frankie called Margot from the office and asked if she wouldn't mind taking Gracie next door and making her some dinner. Margot and Gracie had spent the afternoon colouring Robert's plastic head, so it now had purple hair, red eyes, thin yellow lips, a gold chin, and kind of bruised cheeks where Gracie couldn't decide between green or brown. Frankie said she'd get her P.A. to order Dominos, but Margot made croquettes instead, from sweet potato, cheese, onions, kale and breadcrumbs. It was a dish she cooked every other Friday at school. But there was something strange about cooking in Frankie's home for Frankie's child, something that made her stomach ache a little.

How did Frankie do it? Raising a kid on your own always seemed impossible.

Frankie came home just before six, and Margot left them to it. When Margot walked through the front door, she found Glen in the dining room with a tumbler of whiskey and Robert's multicolour head set out on the table in front of him.

'What the hell is this?' he said.

'Excuse me?'

'I thought printing the head was bad enough, but colouring it like this? It's really messed up.'

'Gracie did it, you idiot. I looked after her this afternoon.'

Glen picked up the head with one hand and looked at it. Not quite the Yorick pose, but close enough.

'It's funny really,' he said.

'What is?' said Margot.

'Love.'

'Oh God, Glen, really? How much have you had?'

'There's this guy in *Spectrum*, called Billy.'

'I know about Billy.'

'He says that the purpose of love is to bring people together and have babies, to reproduce, but it's the having babies that destroys the love. Reproduction equals destruction.'

'And isn't Billy the old psychopath who lives in a cabin with a pet wolf for family?' Margot said.

'Of course he fucking does.'

'And you really believe that? The thing about babies? I'm going upstairs. Can I have the head please?'

Glen pushed himself up out of the chair.

'Don't you think I know why you stayed all these years?'

'Can you just give it here?' said Margot, gesturing at the head.

'By all means.'

Glen drew his arm back and rugby-launched the plastic head across the room, and though Margot shifted her weight and stretched out an arm to intercept, she could only watch as Robert's colourful, carefree face flew past her, rotating ever so slightly in the heavy mid-air, then hitting the kitchen wall and splintering into shards; scalp flying into the sink, chin speeding across the lino towards the living room. Glen looked at his hands like he was seeing them for the first time. Margot fell to the ground and scooped up pieces of her child. Half a yellow lip and the bristle of a brow, the peak of the jawline that once belonged to Glen, clumps of indigo hair, a single watching eye.

She held them close and tight, so close and so tight and, when she shut her eyes, Robert was in her arms again in a warm haze of entonox behind the green curtains of the maternity ward; all pain had gone from the world and the future sparkled with the anticipation of a thousand firsts, and look there, his first smile – though certainly just wind, but a smile indeed on such thin little lips – and then, from somewhere outside the haze, Glen leaned in to cuddle the two of them, and Margot couldn't be sure if his arm was around her on the maternity ward or right there in the kitchen, so she kept her eyes closed until she was sure she was alone again.

Mother and Child

Denise O'Hagen

Flesh and blood, 158.5 x 35 cm, 1997, artist unknown

She sat, like we all did, holding him wrapped in
Soft stripes of pastel pink and blue; you could tell
Those hospital blankets anywhere. The air was

Hushed around her, shadowed like the underbelly
Of a mushroom, painting her in the finest strokes of
Pale grey. I held my own complicated bundle of life

Tighter. Things were precarious, more than any of us
Wanted to admit. The nurses trod back and forth,
Watching us, and the clock; our half an hour was

Nearly up. She looked at me then, her eyes dark bruises
Against the shock of her face, and drew her child to
Her breast, swollen with undrunk milk. The blanket

Slipped from miniature limbs, a plastic anklet. Silently,
She pulled the blanket back and shielded him with the
Full curve of her body, brushing his head with her lips.

She would not give up; she would fill the space left
By his unresponsiveness, and tend that which had
Grown between them during their nine short months:

A portrait of mother love, blocked out there in the ward
In its most elemental form, unyielding in the face of fact.
I recognised myself in her, and shivered; she was all of us.

Woman, Mother, Other

Lucy Pearce

Bones blush with beatings of twelve,
She curls at the corners,
Woven from fragile frame and paper skin,
Rotten teeth and hand-me-downs,
                    "Did you take this, *girl*?"
Then damp, deadened,
Nerve endings burnt into numbness
Dressed in silent smiles and lowered eyes,
Privately pained and publicly vailed,
                    Daughter.
Five fingers frayed at the tip,
Worn from penury, sorrow, slog,
She is laced corsets and pressed seams,
Turned beds and polished gold,
                    House keeper.
From waning wax grows adulation,
Hushed words wrapped in needle lace,
Legs, hips, and ravelled hair,
Sourdough and submission,
                    Wife.
Inside she moulds without mutton,
Scarcely moaning when wood meets frame,
Nine months and life-long,
Sponge baths and crimson palms,
                    Mother.
Shall duties die at her side?
Perhaps in nights of liberated soul,
Of rallied voice and whitened fist,
Of yes and no and yes once more,
                    woman.

In darkness brews the loudest truth,
From painted lips with staple holes,
She is power and undiluted mind,
She is courage, she is sagacity and she is
Woman.

Love Apples
Liz Houchin

Three days after Christmas, in a semi-detached house in Dublin, Barbara laid to rest the carcass of her twenty-third turkey. This was how she measured the passing of time, a much more respectable number than her age. Both her children had brought friends home from college who had nowhere else to be, and she was grateful for their animation and their appetites. They were now gone to drink in the New Year in some unsuspecting country house. Her husband had nipped to the office to check on things, so she finally had the place to herself. She worked from home as a literary agent and spent the morning responding to emails from her authors – a mix of good wishes and existential despair – and over lunch she ordered tomato seeds: *Gardener's Delight*, *Sungold*, and a new black tomato, *Indigo Rose*, because you only live once.

Her love of tomatoes began on a hot July afternoon fifty years previously when her mother, on seeing the shadow of the health visitor at the door, shoved a carton of tomatoes in front of her as she sat on the grass in nothing but a pair of frilly pants. The health visitor had come to see Barbara's baby brother, who had spent his first weeks in an incubator. As she was packing away the tools of her trade, she looked over from the kitchen chair that was moonlighting as garden furniture.

'Well, you'll never need to worry about her appetite,' she said.

Her mother followed her gaze to the orange rivulet running down Barbara's chubby torso and the empty carton resting on her head of blonde curls. For the rest of the summer, anytime she was asked what she would like to eat, Barbara would simply say 'meat and mat,' translated as ham and tomatoes.

Barbara had eaten them almost every day of her life.

Six weeks later, on Valentine's Day, Barbara stood in her ancient greenhouse and turned on the AM/FM radio that still had its original batteries and never minded a dusting of compost or a splash from a watering can. The midmorning presenter was reading out the winning entry to a love poem competition, the subject seemingly a labradoodle named Billy. It was quite touching really.

Barbara got to work sowing her tomato seeds in the same little pots as last year. It was her favourite gardening job; the promise of new life and better weather. She knew they would germinate, as sure as she knew the authors who would turn in their manuscript before the deadline and the ones who would put all their creative energy into excuses and lies, some of which were exceptionally good and could easily have been turned into flash fiction or perhaps a haiku. February was holding on to winter with both hands, and a fierce westerly rattled the fragile aluminium frame that threatened to simply crash to the ground one of these days. Two of the windows were held together with packing tape. Just as she was watering the pots, her husband appeared and coaxed the door open wide enough to pass through a shocking pink orchid.

'Happy Valentine's Day!' he said, flushed.

'Well thank you, this is a surprise.' She put down her watering can and leaned over for a kiss, careful to keep her hands away from his suit.

'I was in the shops and thought you'd like it.'

'You went to a shop? Well there's a first time for everything. I'll just finish up here and get us some lunch. You can tell me all about your adventures in retail.'

'Actually, I have to run back to the office, but I'll be home for dinner.'

She tore the heart printed cellophane from around the

plant and watched him sprint away. While the colour of the flower was mildly offensive, she was grateful for his sudden rush of blood to the head. She felt bad that she hadn't bought him anything, but he valued a good meal above most things. She looked forward to a steak dinner and a glass of wine, but by the time he came home his mood had changed and when she thanked him again for the orchid, he seemed embarrassed, almost like it had been a lapse of judgement that he hoped everyone would have the decency to forget.

A month later, she decamped to the greenhouse on a Saturday morning to transplant the seedlings into bigger pots. Holding one of the first true leaves between her fingers she used an old pencil to lift the white thready roots from the soil and move them to their second home where they would have room to spread out and support five feet of vines. She repeated this action over and over while reading a draft of her favourite author's new novel, covering it in brown thumbprints. It was getting harder to sell books written by people who remembered life before the Internet but this one would be difficult to ignore. She hoped it would remind people that, like the mock orange she had planted beside the front door, some of the most beautiful flowers bloomed only on old wood.

Pausing to turn the page, she noticed her husband on his phone in the shed at the end of the garden. There was no reason for him to be in there and he seemed quite agitated, pacing about as much as anyone could pace in a shed. Their shed was a damp gloomy place where DIY dreams went to die, so Barbara kept her gardening tools in the greenhouse. He must have been aware that she could see him, so that evening she asked him if everything was alright.

'I saw you on your phone in the shed.'

'Yes, yes, just work, trying to persuade HR to bend the rules for a new hire.'

'Right. I thought it was something more dramatic.'

'Colonel Mustard in the shed with a screwdriver. Not everything's a murder mystery you know.'

'I was thinking more along the lines of a suburban thriller – disguised as a middle-aged accountant, a secret agent takes down the head of the residents' association who is, of course, a war criminal.'

'Nothing that exciting I'm afraid. Anyway, I'm going to pick up some notes from the office that I should review before Monday. Need anything?'

On the second Sunday in April, it was warm enough to have lunch in the garden. Barbara brushed down two garden seats for the first time that year and stole a cushion from the kitchen to insulate her behind from the damp. Nothing signaled summer's approach like eating outside. Pointing out new tulips she had planted the previous autumn, or planning a holiday, they would sit and chat and laugh. But not this time. Her husband was just back from a two-day business trip, and all she felt was a tightness in her chest that had been quietly building for weeks. She had considered a rare visit to the GP, but a phone call the previous day had diagnosed the problem and it was time to share. She put down her fork.

'So, when are you going to tell me?'

'Sorry?'

'Yes, you should be, but I doubt you are.'

'What?' he kept his focus on his plate.

'The estate agent called with some good news while you were away. He has someone on his books who is interested in viewing our house. I thanked him warmly. He must have assumed that the house was in both our names and that I knew it was going on the market.' She picked up her fork and returned to her quiche. Her heart was now bouncing off her ribcage.

'Oh Barbara, I was just making enquiries,' he said. 'I was going to talk to you first, but I was waiting for the right time.' He reached out his hand and placed it over hers.

'It's all just happening so quickly,' he softened his voice. 'I didn't plan it. God knows I would never want to do anything to hurt you. It's just one of those things. We met at work and she –'

Barbara pulled her hand away, put her finger to her lips and shook her head. She read books for a living. She had skipped the first few chapters, but she knew how this story ended. She took her cup to the greenhouse and gave all her attention to her tomato plants, pinching outside shoots and tying in stems, wiping away washes of tears with her sleeves. She stayed there until she heard his car leaving.

Three weeks later, she was driving back from the solicitors, her marriage all but over. She had stayed standing during the meeting, refused tea, and used her own pen. She wouldn't know how she felt for a long time. Turning on the radio to drown out the morning, she caught the end of her favourite song from her college days. She wished she could hear it from the start. Barbara had a habit of playing a song again and again until it keeled over. It drove her husband crazy. He would plead with her to play something new. 'But everything I need right now is in this song,' she would explain. It was how she felt in her greenhouse, with potting compost under her fingernails and in her hair, searching for a packet of seeds that she just had in her hand, or finding shoots that had pushed their shoulders up through the dark overnight and were now lifting their heads to the light.

She parked her car but didn't bother going into the house. Straight through the side gate, stripping off her black, don't-mess-with-me jacket and flinging it on a bench. She pulled her earrings from her ears, kicked off her shoes, and slid her feet into a pair of ugly rubber garden shoes that she would like to be buried in. Her tomato plants were now three feet high and covered in tiny yellow stars, but the leaves were drooping and the soil was dry. She started plant triage immediately and swore that nothing else would get in the way of their care.

The house sold without having a sign erected beside the front gate. She was thankful for that, but it meant that she only had a month to leave. Her husband was already holed up with the woman who made him feel young again so he just wanted the cheque. He had also promised the children the panacea of a generous cash gift so lots of helpful pressure was applied to get Barbara out of the house, including a bargain bin mindfulness book entitled, '*Moving on with Joy*'. She mindfully shredded each page and sprinkled them on top of her grass clippings.

She found an apartment that she could just about afford. As she signed on the dotted line, she said a prayer that one of her authors would have a bestseller at some point before she died. She did not canvass anyone's views on the property and couldn't explain why she chose it. Nor would she share her new address widely until she was settled, fearing that a single *New Home!* greeting card would be enough to send her into a deep decline.

Barbara would not accept a suggested late May or early June deadline to leave the family home. Did these people know anything about how tomatoes actually grow? In the middle of June, she fielded phone calls from both her children. Clearly, they had held summit talks. Did they think she was holding out for a reconciliation? She walked out to the garden and balanced her phone on the edge of the compost heap so she could deadhead *Rosa 'Graham Thomas'* while her son and then her daughter expressed empathy tinged with impatience. Barbara counted the wilted roses with each snip and made the occasional 'I'm listening' noise, eventually pressing the mute button and telling them exactly what to do with their concern.

July 2nd. Friday had been her absolute deadline to leave the house, but summer heat had returned, and she needed another 48 hours. Her husband was in Greece so she had simply called the estate agent and said that she needed more time and if they wanted the house they would have to wait until after lunch on Sunday, and no, she wouldn't be answering her phone again.

She woke on the nose of 8.00 am. The day broke quiet – so quiet – and warm. Wandering into the almost empty kitchen, she looked out and saw that the air vents had already opened in the roof of the greenhouse. That was a good sign, but she wouldn't go out yet. She made the last cup of tea she would ever drink in her house. Even with bare walls and most of the furniture gone, it felt like her home. The morning light cast the shape of a sail across the wood floor. By lunchtime it would move to where the table used to be, but by then it would be someone else's light. She drained her cup and got dressed.

She walked out to the greenhouse bringing a big colander and a pair of scissors. Pulling away the brick that held the door closed, she stepped inside, the air filled with the scent of warm, fuzzy tomato leaves – a musty, herby smell with touches of tobacco and lemons. Describing the smell of tomato plants reminded her of a wine tasting event she went to with her husband and how they had giggled every time someone swirled their glass and suggested, '*Fresh tennis balls*'. Like bold kids swinging on their chairs and daring the teacher to kick them out. She leaned back against the potting bench and closed her eyes, committing to memory the feeling of glass-hot sun on her face.

Before the year was out, she would hear reports of her ex-husband's first 10K run. His new partner was a list of everything Barbara wasn't. It hurt like hell, but right now she was busy saving her summer. Her first tomato harvest would be her last. The *Indigo Rose* tomatoes were an extraordinary colour. Not quite black, but the darkest shiny purple you could imagine. Most of them had only started to colour but there was a group of three near the top that were as perfect as snooker balls. The *Sungold* cherry tomatoes hung in long bunches like extravagant Mardi Gras earrings, deep orange baubles at the top and fading to bright yellow and then lime green at the bottom. But the *Gardener's Delight* stole her heart, as they always did. Branches weighed down with deep red picture book tomatoes, every one as perfect as the last. She had an hour before the new owners arrived, so she worked her scissors until the colander was heaving. Then she dragged the pots outside, dumped the plants on the compost heap and walked away.

She placed the colander of tomatoes on the passenger seat, the ripest ones resting on top. Her laundry bag was in the footwell, and her hairbrush was in the cupholder. The boot and backseat were packed with all the stuff the movers didn't move. She left all of her big gardening tools behind, but still planned to arrive at friends' houses armed and dangerous with a secateurs and a pair of gardening gloves ready to put manners on an overgrown shrub. She patted the rim of the colander and drove like she was taking her first baby home from the hospital.

The apartment that was now her home had no balcony, but the sun shone through the kitchenette window for a couple of hours each day, at least in summer. Barbara laid the green tomatoes along the windowsill to ripen in the company of a basil plant. She opened the first box labelled 'kitchen' and found a gold-rimmed soup bowl from her wedding china. Her first instinct was to fling it across the room with the force of an Olympic shot-put champion. But instead, she filled it with orange, purple, and red tomatoes, still warm from the car and ready to burst.

Kicking off her sandals, she hiked herself up on the hot worktop, letting her feet rest in the sink. Barbara liked to know where she stood (or sat) in the world. Out the window, she could see in the distance the red and white striped chimneys of Dublin Port. That meant the Wicklow mountains were straight ahead of her and her greenhouse was behind. She unfolded a threadbare tea towel, laid it across her knees, and let the juices fall.

Proustian Moment

Anna Seidel

This tongue is a petrified dream catcher,
weighed down by an obesity of grief.
A sponge heavy with the salinity of
fifty-thousand scent memories.
Echo chambers; carrying every bruise,
every story, every melody.
For those passed become embedded
like an anchor in our hippocampus
and by chance resume their place
in consciousness.
Hidden somewhere
beyond the reach of intellect,
in olfactory sensation,
for it's the earliest language known.
What appellation approaches
the aroma of grilled corn on the cob
thickening the air in tropical June heat?
And what word fuses this haze
with the sorrow of having lost it?
I want for this taste to inhabit my mind,
be embalmed, anointed by it,
to have something of you in the end.

Sirocco

Donka Kostadinova

Today
I'm wearing the hot
easterly wind –
ribbons of dust
and sand
loop and coil
around my face
until my mouth
becomes the eye
of a storm
you want to kiss

my words halt, stunned
they hide between my teeth –
they go back a long way,
I don't want to lose them

exotic, you want to taste them
smell
try them on
see if they suit your mind
before you commit

your tongue finds a stray –
four syllables to your three,
pin it down on display, spread it –
pretty eyeshadow-winged creature.

you bite it, breast milk dribbles –
   from the corner of your mouth
      Spit or swallow?
         perhaps
            it will it look better
               on the pavement
                  to be trampled –
                     undocumented,
                        it does not belong,
                           a blow-in

         sometimes,
            even I forget,
               no one understands it,
                  not even my children.
                     My mother does.

When I dream, blue poppies soar on my breath.

Up

Neil Tully

Highly Commended

Opening day at Cheltenham and I'm staring through the wall of screens at Ladbrokes, down two hundred quid. Thinking of ways to make some cash so I don't have to limp back to Mags Forde like a kicked dog, with her crooked teeth and thin lips and fingers in every criminal act in the county. Thinking hard, coming up with nothing.

They have a fan on blowing failed slips across the dirty carpet, each one a receipt for hope bought with cash, no refunds. There's been ferocious heat all day. First time I've ever seen the regulars use the water cooler. The smell of sweat is powerful. Working man's sweat, drinking man's sweat, gambling man's sweat. Old Gandalf is propped up on a stool, deep breathing gum disease, looking like he's been waterboarded. The commentary from Turffontein is on low, like some anxiety-riddled narration of life in here.

Sully is watching the dogs. He was up twenty-seven quid, so put a nice round two-euro coin down on trap 4, announcing that it was his final bet of the day. When he walks into Ladbrokes, his wallet tightens like a clenched fist. Smart, I suppose. When you're up against it with the bookie, you're either the hare or the greyhound. The hare, Sully, runs for his life because he's got something worth running for. The greyhound, that's me, does the only thing he knows, and chases even harder. The problem is that today's two-hundred wasn't just the dole, but the last of the three-thousand-four-hundred-and-twenty-seven euro sixty-three cents that Mam left behind in this world. The only thing that was keeping me from Mags' door.

144

I go and stand next to him, a foot bigger up and across, looking like his bodyguard. The longshot trap 4 dog powers home at 9/1, and Sully's eyes light up at the prospect of a wrinkled twenty coming back across the counter. It's Fat Ray working today. He has a back you could play handball off. Pays out any measly winnings as if it's coming from his pocket. Good for Sully. But could he not have thrown on twenty? We'd be off to Longnecks with a hundred and eighty quid, having a few pints and laughs, and I could forget about Mags for one more cider-soaked evening. I could go home drunk enough to fall asleep, without being tortured by Mam's things. Slippers, hair curlers, hand creams. The plastic basket of medicines, bandages and antiseptics. The bottle of years old perfume she'd *treated* herself to and dabbed on as if it was Christ's tears, still saving it long after it was past its best, our little corner of the world never giving an occasion worthy of its use.

Sully goes to collect, and Gandalf leaves with a hacking cough by way of goodbye. Hadn't had a winner all day, same as myself. Think he lives out the straight road, but not sure. See him in here plenty, stroking his beard and never winning, like some unwise mystic.

'Sully, can you spot me twenty? I'll get you back Friday.'

'Course, Mellott,' Sully says.

He's only tight with the bookie. If either of us gets a win over five-hundred quid, we split it, then drink most in celebration. He hadn't even time to pocket his wallet. Opens it up, a few notes colour coded, Tesco Clubcard, imprint of a condom coming through from the back compartment. Been in there so long, it's as likely to stop a pregnancy as a free bar at a debs. He hands twenty over and doesn't expect thanks, just follows me outside for a smoke.

'Bad luck today,' he says.

No further comment is needed, so we squint at the Mayo sky then across the carpark. Still a heavy heat, the Moy across the road sounding cool and tempting. We nod at a couple of fellas who drive by on their way home after another day of digging roads, breathing tar, collecting bins, filling skips and lifting blocks with crippled knees. All those jobs were given to men without degrees. Home to a three-bed semi, kids screaming about bath time. Wife complaining about their snoring when they finally do drift away from it all. Knackered greyhounds. Chased down the hare they were told to, only when they sank their teeth in, they discovered that it was never real. Like the one at the track. While unseen men made the real money, now all they can do is keep running in circles.

Sully won't stay around much longer. He's too smart. His family's too good. Went to Galway and got a degree. He's back working with his auld fella, saving for his escape. Dublin first, I'd say. Then London, then Zurich or Frankfurt or some European hub where he'll wear suits and watches and meet some leggy, tri-lingual Swiss blonde who'll whip any last bit of Mayo out of him. And he'll get home for a few days at Christmas, then only every other year, and eventually his folks will die and he'll forget this county and this town and these people and these days and this warm March evening when every cent to my name came from his pocket.

I'd have gone to college with him if I could. Got the points I needed. Just never had the money and was looking after Mam while she was on her way out. That's what I told myself anyway. That I was tethered to the place by the collar and a cage. That the Creggs Road son of some feral stray, who'd wronged my mother once, doesn't have a way out, isn't bred for colleges or cities or any world beyond this. Never had a reason to think any other way.

'There's one more race if you fancy a last punt? Might come good,' Sully says, his pity as bad as him knowing that the twenty he lent me is all I've left.

I've been tipping Mr Yeats in the 6.15 all day. Gorgeous bay gelding, priced at 50/1. Saw him run 5th a few weeks back and know he has more in the tank.

'Yearah I'll leave it, Sully. Better strike away home.'

I walk off, round the corner, not sure why I'm pissed at him. Not pissed at him. Pissed at everything. Pissed to be headed back to Mags, who picked me from a litter of drinkers in McCrann's one night three years back. Nineteen years old, Sully away at college, Mam not able to sit or lie down without agony because of pressure sores on the back of her thighs. Festering, putrid openings with their hateful stink that I rinsed with saltwater and bandaged and prayed to fuck every morning would look better. I thought maybe Mags knew something of me, was throwing me some work to help out. But she just saw a six-foot-three lad with no job, fists like mallets and nothing to lose. Another dog for her pack.

I put ten euros of petrol in a canister at Maxol. Enough to get the Intruder back to town when I've cash to fill the tank. I walk the high street, taking the long route, as if a way out will land in front of me before I get to her. Shopkeepers pulling down shutters, Frank the butcher sweeping sudsy water out his door, the stink of raw meat coming with it. Oil heating up in the chippie, a woman in the Chinese taking phone orders for dinners. Happy hour in Longnecks, the doors open and music comes out.

She put me to work in a dirty bungalow on the edge of town, six 'til two in the morning. Showing my big, bulky frame in the hallway and snarling at whatever porn addict came in to use the women that were working the rooms. Usually four on rotation, two on days, two on nights. Eastern European, mostly. Once the punter had seen me, I'd go to the back room, making myself scarce in what Mags called her office. Put the takings in a locked top drawer, wrote down the amount each woman had earned in a notepad. Stared at an ashtray overflowing with fag butts for hours on end, while bedposts rattled and fellas came and went, avoiding my eye.

I'd convinced myself for a while that I was just a bouncer. Eventually realised my job wasn't to keep the women safe. It was to keep them in. Keep them profitable. They were captured prey, laid out for all manner of Mayo's dirty dogs, cute foxes and vicious mink.

One night, I got home, and Mam was dead. I'd left her that evening, vomiting, thinking it was the chicken I'd cooked for her lunch. The pressure sores had gone septic, torn through her skin and poisoned her blood. While I was sitting at Mags Forde's desk, counting her money, helping her to trade in the flesh of other women.

Now I'm going back, out the Racecourse Road, tail between my legs, after swearing I never would. Ten quid and a can of petrol, my lot in life. Stink rising from the can. I wonder, can it self-combust in this heat? Send me up in flames by the roadside and maybe I'd be better off.

Mags' bungalow is in sight. Makes my stomach lurch. Her van isn't in the yard, but that doesn't mean she's not in. She has skinny Pat Dwyer driving her sometimes, like she's some visiting ambassador.

The gate is open. I walk the long flank of the bungalow, ugly pebble dash, rusted satellite dish, curtains are drawn. From the outside, every inch is a pensioner's home in need of TLC. I get to the back door and it's all too familiar. Six months since I was here. Give a loud knock and listen for any noise inside. Nothing. A car passes on the road. I knock again, louder. Longer. Heels softened on the lino inside, the blurry shape of a woman through frosted glass.

The door opens. She's late thirties, tired. Brunette. Pink lipstick, some eyeshadow, nothing else on bad skin except a fresh roll of deodorant. She's wearing a dressing gown. Cheap lingerie underneath no doubt. As if a Guard wouldn't spot the six-inch heels.

'Can I help?' she says. No prizes for guessing the accent.

'Mags in?'

'I don't know who you mean,' she says. Well-practiced. Scared stiff. You haven't seen violence until you've seen Mags 'teach her girls a lesson'.

I walk in and she shouts something but stands aside all the same, wary and weary of men my size. No muscle appears. The sparse living room's as grim as I remember. Somebody's added a rickety trolly with cheap bottles of spirits from Aldi. Some fairy lights above the window. Has the same rejuvenating effect as giving Lemsip to a man wracked with bowel cancer.

A younger woman comes into the room, a black bra and a thong, legs as skinny as a deer's. Eighteen at a push. She says something foreign to the woman behind me who's telling me to get out. I see their eyes meet. Eyes so similar, like mine and my mother's, and I turn to the older woman, thinking of the length Mam would have gone to keep me from Mags' reach, let alone serve me up between her jaws.

'Jesus Christ,' I say. 'Is this your daughter?'

I point at the young one and the mother stamps past in her heels, headed for the phone in the office. I follow her in and knock it off the desk, knowing Mags makes them lock up their phones while on duty. I put the can on the desk, and it's either the fumes or the shame or the memories or the thought of the young one in one of those rooms, but my head is spinning. A band of pain working my forehead, jaws pulsing.

'Relax,' I tell her. 'Bloody relax.' I need a second to think.

Rubbing my temples, tugging at the neck of my t-shirt. Feeling like the collar is being yanked and the cage is getting smaller.

Sweat pouring off me, my heart going like a jockey's whip. I sit at the desk, the firmness of the chair against my arse and spine so familiar. Countless nights spent dozing in it. The same ashtray of fag butts, some lipstick-stained, some not. Box of matches next to it. The calendar on the wall still stuck on last September, the spare key for the top drawer taped to the underside of the desk. I go back to that night, sitting here, with Mam dying on her own, vomit on her pillowcase and in her hair, while I looked after Mags' business for a few quid an hour. She didn't even come to the funeral, when I closed the coffin on Mam's gaunt face after spritzing her a few times with her all-important perfume. Didn't even throw an extra fifty my way. Just moaned about having nobody to cover and it being a busy weekend because the Fleadh was on over in Castlebar.

'She's no' here, what do you want?' the older woman is demanding, her dressing gown hanging open to show a faded tattoo on a stretch-marked stomach.

My phone's vibrating in my pocket and I pull it out just as a call ends from Sully. He's sent a text too. I read it, twice.

'Twenty quid win on Mr Yeats! A fuckin grand! get to Longnecks. Half is yours.' I read it a third time, standing up, kicking myself for not sticking around. For not being beside him as Mr Yeats hopped the last fence, jockey and grandstand roaring him on and the pair of us cheering like wildmen in Ladbrokes, Fat Ray seething behind the till. I don't even realise I'm laughing, punching the air and pacing the room.

'What's funny?' she says, no longer scared, just thinking I'm trapped in the head.

'Myself and a pal had a winner at the horses.'

'So you're here to spend it, or no?' she says, hand on hip, getting fed up.

'And give my money to Mags?' I say, shaking my head, tearing the duct-taped key off the underside of the desk, unlocking the top drawer. Taking out the cash box. At a glance, there's about fifteen hundred in it. I cross the room with the stack of notes and the woman's backing against the wall. I hold it out to her. Fair's fair.

'Take this and you never saw me.'

She meets my eye, almost whispers. 'She'll know.' Her face softens, as if she's calculating the risk, glancing over my shoulder at the can of petrol on the desk, knowing what comes next.

I shake my head. 'There'll be nothing left. There's enough here for you to be long gone by tomorrow.'

She nods. Takes the money then turns and scurries away. I hear them scrambling some things together, then racing away to God knows what den they have to hide in, the young one looking over shoulder and meeting my eye.

I unscrew the canister and pour the petrol across the desk and room. Splash it along the corridors where I know Mags' cameras won't pick me up. One above each bedroom door. One above the front door. None in the office of course, where Mags does her business. None at the back door, where her business partners come and go. Out to the living room, emptying the vodka and whiskey and rum around the place.

Back to the office, striking a match and tossing it. Christ, is there a better smell than a freshly struck match? I make sure it takes, none of this walking off with it burning over my shoulder shite you see in films. It catches and the flames stand and stretch and grow and spar and dance. Then I'm gone, out the back door, hopping the back wall, onto the Racecourse Road, headed for town. Getting Sully on the phone, Mags' bungalow bringing the mercury up a notch or two.

'Story, lad?' I say and he's buzzing about the win. Can hear all the chat in Longnecks in the background. Ask him to call me a pint, tell him I won't be long. Knowing it will be our last big winner around these parts. Knowing that Mags will be out hunting. Knowing that I'm free to run, nothing but the open ground in front of me. That I'm the hare now. That I always was. Since I came into this world, ears and nose twitching, nothing for the likes of me to do but survive.

Ménage à Trois

Ekaterina Crawford

There were always three
in this marriage. Me,

> *you*,

and your friend
or so you came to call it.

Hesitant, at first, his visits were rare
and fleeting. Bolder,

> *with time*,

self-assured, he visited more often,
stayed for longer,

> *became more aggressive.*

Aged in Ireland,
matured in Scotland,

> *He claimed*

to know more of the world,
made

> *you*

see things through his eyes, spoke
on your behalf, when you felt tongue-tied,

and made me tremble from your touch.

Meetings, hypnosis, therapy
kept him away for just that long until

one day

I knew –
your friend was here to stay.

We learned to coexist
He and I –
each in our own time.

By day, I still have your love,

but as the sun goes down, your friend
slithers out from his glass lair

as night falls in, I run and hid

Revisiting the Island

Sharon Black

Mull is rain, a washed-out sky,
the gorse's yellow flames long guttered.
I am already lost.

The waterhole is dark brown
flecked with white, I don't know how deep.
They say three feet but my thoughts
don't touch the bottom.
Monks stitched speedwell
into their hems

before they walked a pilgrimage,
now the bright blue flowers
grow along old pilgrim routes.

If this path leads anywhere
then let it bring me loss along the way,
a letting-go of this hard pack,

a setting-free of names.
Dropped seeds.
The island gives me

everything I need and there's nothing
I wish I hadn't said:
everything was true.

But I wish I had said sorry.
I wish I'd said goodbye.
I wish I had said yes.

Walking with William Butler

Jennifer Armstrong

Old Willie takes my hand and walks me slowly up the side of Benbulben. Steep and gravelly, there is danger lurking with every step and misstep. Old Willie is long dead and has no fear of what lays beneath or ahead. He sleeps amongst the lambs that graze and the warrior's bones that have been ground down and trampled on decade after decade. I have a life still to live. I dig my heels deeper into the soil, praying for grip.

He wants to walk up the northern rim, the angle almost vertical straight into the sky. I convince him to take the south side, which meanders more softly into the clouds.

'I want to show you something,' he says, 'while the day is still glorious with sunshine.'

All the while, there is a ringing in my ear. The sound of someone singing in the distance. The melancholy chanting of bleak hymns and doleful refrains.

When I look around, I cannot see another soul. I reckon it must be just old Willie, whispering ditties as usual under his breath. I hear it still as we pass through the fields, which remain wet with dew even though the morning has left. Willie instructs me to reach down and move my fingers through the grass.

'The ground here never fully dries,' he tells me. 'There is a certain texture brought down by the clouds into the atmosphere, which keeps the air moist and the soil damp.'

Willie does not mention the rain. Pouring relentlessly from the heavens.

Willie is old and grey and full of sleep. Despite his eagerness, he can go no quicker than a lame pup. I feel slow myself because, even though the weather is beginning to turn, the wind is harsh at this height and cuts through the skin on my cheeks. It has grown thinner as I have aged and now seems almost translucent.

I am made even more cautious by the unfamiliar ground beneath my feet. It feels different to the dependable soil in the graveyard below, which is made up mostly of decaying bodies and organic matter. The dirt here seems to be undisturbed for centuries, interrupted only with the footprints of the sheep and cattle who roam the fields and guard the mountain.

I have been visiting my dead mother who sleeps in the ground beside Willie, next to the church and the café where they sell claddagh rings and serve quiche. She has been dead for years, but lately it feels as though she has been leaving me slowly, all over again. Without my consent, corners of my mind replay her last moments. It is worst in the mornings when I am still half dreaming – I feel the grip of her fingers around mine tighten and relax. A steady beat, playing out some familiar tune.

Now, I feel Willie's wrinkled hand wrapped around my own, which he squeezes tight when we come upon an unsteady piece of ground. He is whistling an old song and reciting bits of poems.

'I will arise and go now; go to Inisbofin.'

Willie is not well, retreating further by the minute into madness. Verse jumbles in his head, which he splutters out in meaningless rhymes. He is convinced 'the golden apples' are of Ballymun. He picks a dandelion that has gone to seed and blows the feathery strands into the air. He goes on, recalling his aimless decades on these hills, 'wandering lonely as a cloud'.

'That's not even yours,' I protest, but he ignores me.

He drives onwards until we reach a treacherous stony path where we must fall to our hands and knees to creep up slowly like lost dogs.

As we inch forward, he asks about my sadness, and I explain about my mother and how I can feel her around me all the time. Sometimes, I am boiling the kettle in the morning or replacing the toilet paper with fresh roll and the remembering that she is gone hits me anew. Then, it is like the day she died all over again, and I feel a burning pain searing through my chest and my stomach collapsing. Her laugh was infectious, and without her, I have fallen out of the habit. For a while, grief felt like a muscle I had strengthened. But lately, my whole body aches with stiffness, as though every limb has atrophied, and I just want to rest.

Willie offers me a moth-eaten handkerchief from his pocket. He tries to change the subject, reminding me of the beauty of the landscape and the wonderful assault on our senses even now as we climb. The wet grass under our feet and the cold air on our skin, the smell of the moss and the faint whisper on our tongues of salt from the sea. It is hard to take Willie seriously, given his mud-stained green lapels and perspective on life, which has been so altered by his many decades in the afterlife.

'The world has indeed "changed utterly"', Willie goes on, 'and yet, this lovely mound of limestone has not moved nor bent in millions of years. The fossils and bones of the dead sea creatures are still preserved like magic, sewn into these layers of sedimentation.' Willie smiles as he put his hand down to touch the porous stone. 'Hard and unwavering even in the harshest wind.'

I suddenly hear it again despite Willie's tiresome gibberish – the distant voices reciting prayers – but this time, it is more like a choir, singing in a minor key.

We soon come upon a field of lambs, stumbling around like drunkards. Then, further up, the ones born two days ahead leaping about like children in a playground.

'But you once wrote this was all due to end and be destroyed,' I press him after we have walked a while in silence. 'You wrote "the Centre cannot hold", "things fall apart", "the Second Coming was upon us"?'

'Did I really?' Willie looks at me bemused. 'Bah, what do I know.' He pats the head of a rogue lamb who has strayed from its mother. 'We tell ourselves stories in order to live.'

'That's Joan Didion's line,' I object.

'Ah well, she nicked one of mine too.'

A farmer begins to follow us and his lambs, which have strayed, chasing them over the low stone wall where he falls and shouts obscenities. We run until we are far away from his land, though it is indistinguishable from the rest and still full of the same soil and bones. We stop to take a rest, to look out over Sligo town, which appears just a cluster of tiny shacks.

Willie points to a gathering of people on the north side of town, near the turn for the hospital. I tell Willie it is Connolly's Pub, where they are serving takeaway pints and drams of whiskey. He licks his lips and slowly moves his finger westward to the tall grey statue outside the Ulster Bank.

'It's you,' I tell him.

He says nothing, but straightens his back before we move on, fixing his tie and brushing the dirt from his trousers. We turn to the ocean then, to gaze across the piece of land jutting out into the sea – the last stop before New York, my mother used to say.

I tell him about his summer home at Elsinore in Rosses Point village, and how it sits now just as abandoned blocks of stone, covered in cages to keep the strangers out, a piece of history being let wear and run down to ruins. Once more, the lines on his brow deepen.

'Tear it down,' he eventually utters with a dismissive wave of the hand. ''Tis nothing but a pile of old stones.'

'Now honestly, we must hurry on,' he urges, 'we are already late.'

Finally, we reach the summit and sit down for a long rest before we begin to stroll across the flat top of the mountain. My head begins to whir with the altitude, and my stomach feels light, like I am riding a rollercoaster of endless loops.

Willie looks across at Knocknarea and poses as though firing an arrow in the direction of Maeve, standing upright in her tomb prepared eternally for duel. He lends her a graceful bow, conceding before beginning.

'I do not have the strength to take on the Queen', he smiles, 'she has centuries on me'.

I begin to stumble, low on sugar and mouth dry. I nearly trip over the loose stones below into a marshy pool full of spawn. I am struggling to keep up with Willie's nonsense, which is doing nothing to alleviate the heavy pressure mounting in my chest and the dense air stifling my lungs.

But still, he goes on.

'All in all, Sligo looks grand,' he nods as he purveys the scene. 'It still seems to be nestled safely away between the two auld peaks. The Garvogue as well, I can see now, continues to gush into the salty water of the bay, full of swans and mallards fighting for bread.'

'Longer days are on the horizon', he muses as he clasps his hands behind his back and motions me onwards. 'Look there, the grounds of Lissadell House covered in layers of bluebells, almost the colour of a violent indigo tide rushing into the dunes, distinct only from the sea by their scent, which wafts across to the sailors, floating on the waves by the Lower Rosses.'

I look across in amazement. The bluebells had not been there days before, but now when I turn my head, it is all I can see, fields of them flooding into the Hazelwood. Willie walks on as I pinch the skin around my wrist to try and get the blood flowing again to the tips of my fingers, blue with cold and dry against my palms. Soon, we have walked the entire length of the tabletop mountain. Below us stretching down is the curved edge of the cliff, which from Sligo town looks like the yawning tongue of a tired collie.

Willie asks me to sit next to him and dangle my feet over the drop which falls almost 2000 feet. I step backwards, but still, he beckons me forward and tells me to look to the left to Sligo town, glistening now the sun is out. Straight ahead, the sea as calm as glass, but no doubt as cold as Christmas morning. He is unrelenting in his efforts until, finally, I succumb, sitting on the stony ground to his left, curling my legs up under my arms.

'It is quite a sight, isn't it?' Willie exclaims.

I am about to beg him to shut up, but when I turn, he has laid straight back and is already dozing, cheeks angling up towards the sky.

Instead, I am startled by the eyes of my mother, sitting on his right-hand side gazing back at me. I wonder what she is doing here, because I am sure I watched her myself being lowered into the ground at the bottom of this hill. She wakes up Willie and says we must get ready.

'We are already running late,' she says.

She is entirely familiar, even the smell of her perfume and talc floats towards me with the breeze. Her eyes are the same deep shade of blue which, in the natural light of the sun, go green around the rim. I want to stand up and make my way back down the south side, but my legs feel heavy and hard like the stones below.

My mother takes my hand in hers and I can suddenly sense

it then, the feeling of heavy soil closing in around my body. I am overcome with satisfaction, and the comforting feeling of the soft satin cushion which is grazing the skin of my neck. I feel the density of the ground, which surrounds me, down by the church, lying side by side with my mother and Willie, making acquaintances with dead souls and the vegetation of the Spring. I notice a beautiful lightness in my bowels and no longer feel an ounce of hunger. My mother and Willie gaze out towards the sea before both turning slowly to face me, expressions calm and expectant. I realise then why we have come all this way.

Old Willie gets up and walks around so he is on my left, so I am sat between them both, my fingers locked tightly into theirs. We glance down into the plummeting bottom below and I close my eyes in fear, but somehow, I can still see perfectly – the town and beaches and mountains laid out before me. We begin to maneuver our bums gently over the edge, like cautious children on a playground slide. For an instant, I want to scramble back inwards, away from the cliff and the steep drop, as something reminiscent of a heart pounds in my chest. But it is much too late for that now. The beating heart has left me, and inside I am only air. When I look down, I see we are floating weightless by the ledge, and then we are not floating at all.

As we go down, my skin – a moment ago cold and thin – begins to grow full of heat. It becomes covered in the creamy particles of the low hanging clouds. Somehow, the sharp edges of the stones and deep grooves in the rock feel like duck feathers on my bum. We go so fast the breeze takes the breath from my lungs, and even then, I can only laugh as the cold wind is blurring my vision. I see nothing but a haze of colours, mostly green and blue. Some yellow from the flowers and grey from the houses, still brimming with life.

I let go of Willie's hand and gather bunches of daffodils,

which flood the fields we pass. At the bottom, I am still holding my mother's hand, but she is lying backwards in the grass facing the sky, smiling madly at the sun.

'Soon, they will be gone,' Willie says, glancing at the daffodils in my hand, which have already begun to wilt, 'because I'm afraid Spring has lasted long enough.' He brushes the dirt from his jacket as he begins to stroll back up towards the summit. 'But then, of course, the summer will come, and the raspberry bushes will begin to bear fruit which will be sour and sweet and burst on your tongue.'

'People will rob them from the fields, and the pink will stain their lips and teeth as though they have all been mad with kissing, like teenagers in love.' My mother gives a hearty laugh that I can feel echo deep down in my belly.

I do not know how long we spent falling, it might have been forever – I might still be falling now.

Asylum

Anna Seidel

Crossing my lips, you trace each crest, crease, bend,
the branch jabbed soles of my bifid tongue,
feel thin mountain air sped breath-beats;

Explore raw paths plied in soil, riptides of my mouth,
where prayers of poison, prayers of thorns
near childhood dreams rest;

Where secret thoughts silently take seed,
cradling lost roots on taste buds,
hiding a grief finely sewn into flesh.

Did you find the words that had flout borders,
smuggled in the cavities of my wisdom teeth, tunnels
through which memory haunts my mind
like an endless reverberation tremor?
Did you ever have to measure a word's ballast?

These exiled idioms held so much for so long.
Wrapped in sheepskin, vowels crammed,
their lettered backs broken from all the weight.

In each cavern of a kiss, I search foreign words
to re-sculpt my story from, seek harbor
in strange tongues, that so often fail to hold.

Eastern

Elena Croitoru

Was God ever tempted to leave the world
unfinished, I say while we climb a hill

& dig our nails into the hot, aerated ground
surrounded by half-devoured cedars & pines.

My mother stands still as though she is
one of the mannequins that de Chirico

painted, though without the visions
of something better around the corner

of a building with arched windows. The soil
can barely remember the feel

of water, so in a few decades,
nothing will move here. The holes

in the ground are collapsing
in on themselves, over exhausted ants.

Creatures don't rot here,
instead, the water comes out

of their bodies. The constant gunshots
make me think we're in a western though

the shootings out here always mean
something because some of us

won't let anything go & the rest of us
try to fix whatever we can until one day

we learn to run, far from our watchful cities,
where they glued posters of men's faces

over dilapidated murals as if our houses
could be held together by paper

& far from the market, with its brittle walls,
its mounds of softened grapes & hungry dogs.

The mountainscape ahead is shrouded
in a veil of clay dust as if

I'm not living but reminiscing
inside a monochrome photograph, trapped

behind an impossibly strong resin film.
It's just an ordinary life, I think,

with us always in the middle
of someone else's ruin.

Reunion

Bernie McQuillan

You should have come away with me.

That's what his postcard said. The only one he ever sent her
from Los Angeles and a month after they'd split. Fiona wasn't
going to reply anyway, but the fact that there was no return
address was bloody typical of Johnny. And now he was back,
dropping into their university caving club's 20th reunion as
if he'd just left, his arm strung around some girl with gazelle
legs that came up to Fiona's chest. What was left of it when
she took the padding away.

    'Aimee' he'd called her, or perhaps it was just Amy,
her name elongated on his Californian tongue. He talked
enough for both of them, which was just as well because
the girl looked bored, as if a pre-dinner expedition through
Fermanagh's finest cave, Pollnagollum, wasn't her idea of a
fun night. Of course, Johnny was already tunnelling through
the first passage at the front of the group, needing to show his
former gang that he hadn't lost his bottle. The nurse in Fiona
wouldn't just leave the abandoned girl stranded at the cave
entrance though, so she had given her a demo, tightened her
harness, and watched Amy's confident abseil down to the first
pitch below.

    'Ok I'm down.'

    The rope tensed as Amy released her harness, her
suddenly sassy voice rising upwards, competing with the roar
of the Cladagh waterfall. It thundered past Fiona, its spray
soaking her face and dripping down her back through a gap in
the borrowed wetsuit. She'd lost weight in the wrong places
and her scrawny neck wasn't her best look, especially next to
Amy who wore her suit like a second skin. Still, Fiona thought

as she pulled the rope back up, she couldn't help but admire the girl's chutzpah. How different to the way she had been at that age.

It was only when she clipped her line onto the harness for the descent that she discovered her hands were numbed in the chill. As she swung out into the darkness, her fingers slipped off the karabiner and she descended too fast, cursing loudly. Her feet couldn't get a grip on the slimy rocks and her nostrils flared with the pungent smell of the wild garlic in the moist cracks of the limestone. She hung there, quivering like a pendant in the Chateau Marmont.

'Are you alright?'

Amy's accent was pure West Coast, suggesting lazy days on Venice Beach, rollerblading to Santa Monica, and drinking cocktails in the back street bars until dawn. Fiona has stayed in the Chateau once on a work trip to Los Angeles, years after she and Johnny had split. She'd had notions of casually bumping into him on the street until she discovered that no one walked anywhere in that city. Then she'd rung around as many start-ups as she could find, but no one knew him. She'd given up on him then and moved to England and started again, training to be a nurse.

'I'm fine, thanks!' Fiona's voice, as firm as the former matron in her could muster.

She gave Amy a thumbs-up and, ignoring her shaking hands, edged slowly down. Already, the cold was sapping her strength. Her thighs squelched as she moved. How many times had she done this cave without incident, but she'd failed today in front of her ex-boyfriend's girlfriend?

It was hard to believe that it was only 24 hours since she'd been in her office in Saint James's Hospital, looking out over the red-bricked infirmary to the black gates and the two wheezing patients in their dressing gowns, smoking in the damp grey evening. She'd thought about going out and shooing them back onto their ward, but she could understand why they preferred to be outside. Sometimes the hospital felt like a prison, she thought, glancing at the Director of Nursing sign on her open door.

It had taken ten years and long hours of training, but she had finally managed to cast Johnny out of her life. Rising to the top of her profession, she'd wanted to prove to herself, or maybe to him, that she didn't need him.

Bit by bit, over the second decade, the job had taken over her life. Every morning, her heels would clip past the wakening wards to the office block, before anyone else was in and the only milk in the fridge was rancid. She'd pour it away, the cloud of it clinging to the base of the sink, and head instead to the hospital canteen for a cappuccino.

Sometimes, staff would recognise her from her tours of the wards, taking royal visitors for their photos with the cutest children marred only by their nasal cannulas. The kids selected were sickly, but never damaged enough to make you look away. A bit like herself. The chemotherapy had wiped her out and she knew she needed a rest. The reunion invitation had come at just the right time.

'You didn't need to wait for me,' Fiona said, her voice sounding clipped and defensive, the way she sometimes heard the nurses mocking her in the corridors.

They stood together for a minute on the rocks, listening for sounds from the rest of the group, Fiona trying desperately to remember which way to go. From somewhere to the left, she caught Mike's low, steady tone and Ciara's giggles, and she signalled for Amy to follow her. Amy smiled at her.

'I don't think this is really your thing either,' she said.

Fiona tunnelled slowly through to the next cavern, the passages tighter than she remembered, her head filled with the sound of her own laboured breathing and her helmet hitting against the roof. They finally caught up with the others in the first chamber. The pin-pricks of light from Fiona's head torch picked out the mud-spattered faces perched on the black boulders and the water dripping from the glistening stalactites.

She listened to Liam telling Mike excitedly about the cavern he'd stumbled across last year, the rocks covered with flowstone, the entrance tunnel as smooth and curved as his tonsils, and it was as if he'd found gold. And in that moment, in the sheer joy that Liam had experienced, Fiona felt more lonely than she ever had before.

She had flown to Belfast that morning, hired a car and driven down the almost empty motorway, calling in to see her elderly parents in the Clogher Valley. She's told no one here about the cancer. At the time, work had been a distraction and she had buried herself in it after her chemotherapy sessions. No wonder her office felt more like her home than her own flat. She'd ignored the dry cough that had returned in the last month, the queasiness she put down to another damaging external investigation into maternity services. No one asked her how she was really feeling behind the lipstick and the short sleek re-growth, not even the oncologist, and so she never had to lie. After the last scan, her oncologist had been encouraging, telling her things were looking good. He couldn't say anything definite until the results were in, but still.

The caving club members had gathered at lunchtime in their old haunt in Blacklion on the Irish border. Walking into Gallagher's was like being nineteen again, with the yellowed clippings of snooker finals and angling championships papering the smoky-coloured walls. Old men in cloth caps were glued to the faux leather bar stools under the green and black taps of Smithwick and Guinness kegs. There were fewer old men left now and, of course, the Guards no longer stood on the unmarked border waving you through after a night's drinking. The thin, beaky-nosed one used to lean right into

Ken's car, squeaking. 'You're all as full as kites, I could set fire to ye.'

Caroline was perched on a bar stool, all in black, still in thrall to the goths. Beside her, the jutting cheekbones and weathered face of Ken. Fiona had heard that he'd joined the British army, done a couple of tours in Afghanistan, and had a breakdown. He had been parcelled off with a military award and a late diagnosis of post-traumatic stress disorder that had left him with a facial tic and explosions of anger.

Beside him, the soft Armagh tones of Liam, his violin case propped against the bar, the Guinness moistening his throat for the heavier session later. Then Mike and Ciara, the only couple from back then that had lasted. Ciara made silver jewellery now, with amethyst stones the colour of the rock pools, and Mike, who worked in the outdoor pursuits centre, a million miles away from his degree in engineering. They'd known what they'd wanted from the start and hadn't hung about. Their kids were already at university, and they were beginning their new life of semi-retirement, mountain climbing and building a cabin somewhere in France. Ciara had that sort of glow that sun beds couldn't give you, not that Fiona had been back on them since the link to cancer was established.

After a few minutes rest, Ken and Johnny led the way, climbing down steep descents and squeezing through tighter passages. Fiona limped now at the back behind Liam, having jarred her knee against an unexpected boulder. Amy powered ahead. Even the swim across the freezing lake between two chambers didn't faze her.

Fiona's thoughts wandered to the hospital board meeting that she was missing, the promises her Chair would be making on her behalf that he knew she couldn't deliver. She had been the chief nurse for a decade, and, in her weariness, she wasn't sure that she had anything more to give to her patients, to her team and to herself.

They descended further and Fiona crawled more slowly, like the endoscope trawling her body last Christmas, searching for the invading army of cells and finding them in her lymph nodes. The only other person around the office on New Year's Day, the day before her double mastectomy, was the dark-haired domestic, Nicole, just back from her family in Paxos. Full of excitement after her acceptance onto the nurse training programme, she had brought Fiona some Vasilopita, baked by her mother as thanks for the help she had given with Nicole's application.

'She wants you to come and stay on the island,' Nicole said, cutting a chunk of the cake and offering it to Fiona. 'I told her you never see the sun.'

Nicole shared the photos of the turquoise waters beyond her mother's kitchen where the extended family were gathered at the laden table after her grandmother's funeral. When Fiona bit into the cake, her tooth hit a small silver coin and Nicole told her that this would be her lucky year.

As they trudged on, and Fiona slipped further and further behind, she thought about those television programmes she had started watching late at night when she finally went home, where people relocated to remote smallholdings. All they did was hoe and weed and protect their chickens from intruders, but the experience seemed to fulfil them in ways that Fiona had not understood initially. Their lives seemed to improve when their worlds shrunk, whereas she had spent years expanding her world, seeking happiness by reaching out to more and more people. She had hundreds of followers on her social media accounts and had to keep feeding the beasts, thinking up different ways of saying the same thing. It had become work, this twenty-four-hour media presence, alongside the great burden of responsibility for the patients and the staff. These people on television were full of joy in their new, simpler surroundings. Recently, she found herself wanting to emulate them.

It was the sort of fulfilment she had imagined came from having children. At one point, she had anticipated that life with Johnny, her calm steadiness mixed with his charm. But she no longer had the energy for that. Instead, she imagined an alternative life, maybe living on the Greek islands, drinking frappé at a beach tavern and watching the sun set over the bright blue fishing boats nestling in the harbour. Not looking behind, nor ahead. Just being. Enjoying life.

Finally, she emerged, exhausted, into the deepest chamber with its creamy calcite curtains and the jagged teeth of the stalagmites like a giant's smile. No one had noticed her absence. A line from Yeats' poem came to mind as she leaned heavily against a rock, one that Fiona hadn't thought about in years: '*I hear it in the deep heart's core.*' She thought about Yeats' grave at Drumcliffe, not forty miles from where they stood. His remains might even have leaked into the mountain water that flowed down into Glencar Lough and through the cave system into this passage, just like the soul of Nicole's grandmother on her journey to paradise.

Caroline produced bars of chocolate from the emergency box and passed around cartons of juice. Fiona's feet squelched in her ruined trainers. There was a steady hammering in her head. Her arms were so cold and weak, she could barely lift the drink to her mouth. She watched Amy move away from Johnny to examine the rock pearls shimmering in the far corner.

'Did you ever think you should have come away with me?' Johnny was beside her, his thighs not quite touching on the rock, his breath filling the space between them.

In the light from her head torch, she saw how straight and white his teeth now were, so different to the crooked smile he'd had before, the one that had caught her attention that very first day at university.

She wanted to say something witty, maybe even something honest, but when she searched her mind, nothing was there, only utter weariness. She had thought about him for years after he'd taken off, wondering if it could all have been so different. And what had they fallen out about anyway? Whose career was more important, something like that. She wanted to say it was irrelevant now. Too much water under the bridge. She began to feel even colder, and she started to shake, unable to get a word out. Her throat ached and the dry hacking cough returned, echoing around the chamber.

'Dad, come and see this!'

Johnny's hand brushed against Fiona's arm as he moved away. Across from her, Fiona saw Caroline and Ken exchange glances, and she knew they were thinking the same thing as herself – Johnny hadn't waited about, then, if this girl was his daughter. Ken passed her his hip flask and she lifted it to her lips and drank something like brandy that shocked her cough into submission and made her throat sting. She felt the searing heat hit her belly and pain radiating throughout her body.

It was a few moments before she realised that Caroline was asking her if she was all right. She couldn't speak, only shake her head. She watched Caroline signal to Ken that it was time to go. They were, Ken said, suddenly purposeful, exiting by a different route. She could hear it in his voice, some reminder of life on the edge, ricocheting between survival and disaster. She followed him, listening to Caroline's soft words of encouragement behind her and silently weeping when, after climbing upwards for half an hour, a shaft of light shone obliquely into the cave. They came out into the fading summer night and the loud chirping of the crickets. Fiona collapsed onto the grass, gasping in the air.

'You were fantastic,' Ken was saying to Amy, 'for a first

timer. You put us all to shame.'

When they were changed and back on the bus, Fiona checked her mobile. There was a message from her oncologist telling her to ring the hospital urgently. Any time, day or night. She looked up and saw Johnny watching her, a smile playing on those perfect lips. Later in Gallagher's, he said she was the first to know that he was leaving California. Amy was going to university in London in September. He was selling up, finalising his divorce, getting ready to live again.

'It's time for a change,' he said, his eyes on her face. 'I'm coming home.'

Fiona nodded absently, warming her hands on the hot whiskey, her mind full of Nicole's photographs and her mother's offer of a bed on Paxos. She knew that, up close, the Aegean was the deepest hue of aquamarine. She would explore the caves at Amphitrite, diving through the sea's emerald green, cobalt, and navy blue depths.

Not for her the stark grey rock of Yeats' grave and the sodden Fermanagh hills but the gypsum-covered underworld of the sea goddess. Her reddened fingers tightened around the glass, and she knew that, from now on, she would only live in colour.

'I'm coming home, too,' Fiona said and tipped her whiskey glass to his.

Zimbelstern

Charles Penty

("The Zimbelstern *is a traditional organ stop,
originating in Europe, especially Germany, from the 16th
century.
The name means literally 'tinkling star' in German,
and describes it perfectly..." – Tony Firshman)*

Mr. Jacques was the man
who came to do my father's books.
Not once did those companions mark down
any item in the wrong column.

On Thursdays, he'd play the organ
unfailingly, including the time when
his own last illness was diagnosed,
to a congregation of ghosts

at Checkley that only he could see:
The *seventeenth-century vicar*
turning pages of a *Bible* slowly,
Spode Works potters killed by silicosis

mouthing a verse of *Rock of Ages*,
the *spectral lady* knitting a shawl
to wear at her own funeral.
Curious, I once asked about

the famed *Cowled Abbot of Croxden*,
but he said that entity
had not been seen since 1930,
(then rehearsed *Night on Bald Mountain*,

to play for the Kardecist Society up Hanley.)
To the organist, one last, dumb question:
Did the friend for whom you filed the returns
also manifest spontaneously?

If he had, would you have told me?
At Christmas, in both men's memory,
we pulled out all the stops to hear
a *Zimbelstern* splice the cracked air.

My Love, My Violin

Martyn Smiles

O dolce, dolce, My Love,
let us play a little longer,
con expressione, con brio,
sometimes allegro
– ah allegro, allegro assai!
Sometimes far more slow.
You might say lento, largo.
No, no! Rather: adagio

O dolce, dolce, My Love, with you
I'm animato and appassionato.
Let me hold you again fermato, feroce
and hold you messa di voce,
until your neck and breasts
are ben marcato,
or, as some might note
– though I hope none know-
in a pattern most bizzaro.

O My Love, My Violin,
in the right hands
you are a lover above all others.
But in the grip of some just a poor drum,
while others still can only scratch out a screech
– each convinced he is The Maestro.

Love, Rapture Divine,
is mine – all Mine! –
with the ease of a glissando,
when you are in my arms
and my heart is played pizzicato.
You hear my heart's tone
grow louder each and every day
until… eventually?
No, not finale,
but da capo.

Spread Those Wings and Fly

Hannah Storm

You text to tell me there's a moth trapped in your tractor, and you've never seen one like it, and I know it must be special since you were farming these fields long before we met. But just as I am trying to come up with some smart-arsed response, the dots on my phone spring to life again, and I think about what you said about how I can never just send one text, and so I hold my breath as your virtual smoke signal takes shape.

'Come and see it, set it free,' you message, and I want to ask why you think I can do this better than you, working as you do every day outdoors, knowing the form and name and sound of things I never knew before you shared them with me.

I think about your fingers, pitted with soil and oil, your skin rough and rusted with the cold and the years, those hands I have studied so much, and I know you think they might be too harsh, and I wish I could tell you there is no chance of this, because you care more than anyone I know.

There is no time for me to send my second text. I run along the road in my impractical pumps, past the derelict pub, then the farmyard and graveyard, weaving around rusted machinery framed with wildflowers and headstones garlanded the same. On another day, I might pause to read the tributes engraved with the names of people I never knew, many you did, and I might marvel at the metal remains that are just as much a memorial to lives past as the graves of those men and women buried nearby. On another day, I might hover at our old haunt, standing in front of the boarded-up windows, remembering how I dragged out my final glass before going home drunk on regret that we never quite found the right words; how, even later, I would drink to forget the wrong man.

I am forced to slow down across the track that leads past ponies and brambles where last week the poppies rose to knee height, and now the stubble scratches my leg. I think about checking my face in the phone, accustomed to seeing too much of myself on calls that never take me beyond my office walls and yet, somehow, connect me with a world, although never like the one you have shown me.

But I push my phone deeper into my pocket.

When I am with you, I rarely worry how I look. With you, I have never felt so much at home as here, far away from where I fled. Still, when I arrive in the field you're cultivating, you laugh because I am out of place in my skinny jeans and smart jacket, straight off some Zoom thing with people on the other side of the planet, and I am embarrassed this is the bit of me you see now, embarrassed that I don't know what it means to cultivate a field, and that I climb the tractor's metal stairs with nothing like the ease you display around these parts.

I want to show you I belong in your world, so I pull myself up into the cab and sit for some time, taking in your view, and it is more lovely than I imagined. I wait for my breathing to slow, watching the winged insect, which doesn't move from its spot above my head. It is merged into the canvas, and you whisper – although it is only you, me, and the moth, and there is no chance of us being overheard – asking me again to release the fragile flying creature, as if it is the only thing needing to be freed.

'I've never seen anything like it,' you say, and you're looking from me to the moth, and I want to invite you in here with me, to sit next to this insect, because I know there is space here for us all.

'Me neither,' I answer, watching how you watch me, remembering those early nights; how you waited in the corner of the snug, speaking to me when the others had turned their backs, telling me they didn't mean 'nowt' by the way they laughed, just that I was a 'rare breed' here, and how, even then, I didn't mind that you spoke to me this way, as if I was part of your world already; you, the only one of the local lads who made me feel as if I might one day belong.

The moth is still on the grey fabric above your seat, the same shade as the material, and I hold my breath as it opens its wings. Beneath the marbled dark, I see a triangle of red. I know what red means in nature, it is danger and desire, and as I watch it reveal its hidden centre, I think about how it is almost the same shade as my hair, how my appearance has brought both pleasure and pain, and how there have been times when I wish I could have camouflaged myself too. I think about the other man I met that night I met you, how he told me he had always had a thing for red heads and asked if it was true what they said about us being feisty. I think about how he saw me as a rare breed, one to be captured, wings pinned.

Slowly, I reach for my phone and hold it underneath the insect's outstretched body, capturing its image and nothing more. Then, I try to cup my hands around this creature, not wanting to hurt it, worried about its reaction, and I want to ask you if there is such a thing as a moth effect, and if it is similar to the butterfly effect where the beat of a creature's wings provokes a reaction far away.

But now, the moth slips my fingers, and I can almost not bear to watch it throw itself against the window time and time again. I feel the heat rising and wonder if it senses this too. I know the warmth means one thing for one of us and something else for the other, and that perhaps one is better suited to withstand it, at least for now.

Watching it thrash, I try not to think about all the times I tried to escape; when I begged the glass to crack simply so I would have something to show for the pain. I try not to think about the way animals acclimatise to pressure, and how little we notice the incremental increases in temperature. I try not to think about the red flags I missed from the other man I met back then.

Instead, I focus on how it felt to escape back here, the pandemic permitting me to move home, putting a halt to my own carbon footprint as I clipped my working wings, enabling me to explore new worlds and old ones; new words and old ones too, and how I felt that new-old time finding you still here, unchanged, though you would say otherwise. Seeing the moth, I cannot help but wonder how it might feel to bask, opened winged in the warmth and light of you.

We are both silent, watching this tiny thing, willing it to freedom, wanting to spirit it towards the horizon, reeling each time it grazes the glass.

I wait for it to calm. Then I place my hands, cradle-like, across its closed body, feeling its wings whisper my palms. I hear you breathe with relief, but for a few seconds I wonder if it was me, not you, until I realise we both exhaled at the same time.

Now I turn towards the field, lean against the metal handle I used to haul myself up into the cab, and unfurl my fingers. As I open my hands, the moth flies off.

You watch it, wondering, 'How can such a fragile thing have such force?'

'I don't know,' I answer.

'I think you do,' you say, while I lower myself down the ladder.

You are so close, I can feel you, though I know this is still impossible, and I wonder if your presence next to me causes subtle changes in the earth's atmosphere – how else to explain this shift within; the way my insides flutter and the fine hairs on my skin awake to the air's embrace.

My hand is cool against my phone and if you notice it shake you do not tell me, so I turn the screen towards you, wishing it was my face, and show you the photo I took because you have no camera on your phone. On the tip of its right wing there is a tiny missing diamond, torn from the brown. My first reaction is to blame myself, to think I hurt it, hoping to set it free. The damage is easier to see in the photo where the wings are wide. Camouflaged against the canvas, the insect appears intact.

'It's not your fault,' you tell me. 'It must have damaged its wing trying to escape. You took this before you let it go.'

This is how I realise I was right to come back after all these years, but years of shielding myself stop me from saying so now.

'Do you remember the night we met?' I ask instead. 'How you all teased me for being posh, but then you stood up for me and told the lads it wasn't my fault I didn't know the difference between hay and straw?'

You hold my gaze and it is almost impossibly intimate. I have never felt your touch, but now I feel it all.

'How could I forget. The most beautiful and brilliant girl I have ever seen. She flies into our local, perches next to me, that night and the next and the next, and I felt so stupid in front of her, coming from her world with all those words.'

I want to reach out to you but am scared of where we will find ourselves.

'And how I tried to impress her by explaining the difference between dried crops and dried grass and which was the better bet, when I should have explained the difference between the two men who were mad for her – tried to convince her the one she was about to run off with would be less reliable than the one who would stay.'

'I should have listened,' I say, but I am scared it is too late, worried that sometimes you look at me and laugh and say you don't know how you could possibly teach me a single thing after all the places I have been. Sometimes I wonder how I will ever find my place here, and if we will ever be able to tell the difference between the *what is* and *what ifs*.

And so, I seek sanctuary in someone else's words, in the science, searching Google for a moth with red under its wing, and up pops the image on my phone, exactly the same but for the damage. My phone informs us these are more common further south. That they fly in spring, but neither of us mentions how we are at the opposite end of the country and calendar. It is September and summer is near its end.

'Do you know, some butterflies and moths migrate by 10 kilometres a year,' I say, searching for something concrete. 'Something to do with climate change, I suspect.'

You nod, moving closer, and I know we are both feeling for the words to explain why I have returned after so long.

'I wish I could rewind time,' you say.

I do too, but stay silent as you tell me of the changes you have seen to the fields and flowers, to the birds and butterflies – the shifts in the seasons; winters harsher, summers where you can no longer predict the weather with the guides handed down by farmers for generations.

'I wish we had met when we were younger. Then I could have seen it all with you, shown you it to you. It's much harder describing the big changes now when you see things day by day.'

I nod. I'm certain we both know we're not really talking about global warming, unless it is the heat between us now.

'That's some distance over fifteen years,' you whisper, and I remember we were talking about the migrating moth. I know, for all the words we share, we may know what might have been if I hadn't flown away before.

'Moths usually come out at night. Unlike butterflies, they rarely appear by day,' you tell me, as I search into the distance, wondering how far the red underwing has reached already.

'When they do, it means they are looking for warmth, or a mate. But perhaps that was how things used to be. Maybe things are different now.'

I feel your finger settle on my shoulder, the softest of touches, an insect alighting. You trace a line from my collar down, drawing the shape of a wing on my back.

Dotted Line

Milie Fiirgaard Rasmussen

A thought popped into my head that night
       when you were drunk, throwing up
            and having a fight with yourself.
That's all well and good – True,
but then the thought that I kinda wanted to
          kiss you?

I'm blaming the wine,
as you drunkenly attempt to make the bathroom wall recline
       like an airplane seat –
       you complain about heat
          on your cheek,
as I remove the dirty socks from your feet,

There's a time and a place –
       I've got impulse control, although,
I'm sure that my face would
give a peek of my soul –

If we weren't so drunk – my braid has come undone.

I stare at your hair –
it's so long, it's so lush,
       I swear it's the alcohol making me blush.
       Your hair really is pretty –
          all the curls down your back –
             right where your bra's about ready to snap…
Wait, no! I mean, it's just cute,
looks fab – Shit.

I think the Somersby was heavenly –
        it messed up my mind though.
Thoughts like these are endless;
it's quite easy to find yourself
        caught up in a moment – you know what I mean?
It's a side of myself, I hadn't yet seen.

You know..? I hope –
        Or, nevermind – it's a joke
how I can't distinguish a relation;
I have a very shaky foundation.
        It should be straight forward, a straight line,
        straight ahead
but you're a dot in this spot – Maybe I misread myself?

I don't actually know where I'm going with this –
        I digress, it's just stress, probably?
I should really just talk less.

The Owl Man

S. P. Thane

Did you ever hear of The Owl Man?
WHO?
The Owl Man!
WHO?
Who is The Owl Man, to whom it may concern?

He who does not hide
He only lives in the hood of night
He walks with thoughts, wonders and ponders
On top of the trees and everything under

So, have you heard of The Owl Man?
The Who?
The Owl Man!
The Who?
No, The Owl Man, although I like their tunes
Who is the The Owl Man, to whom it may concern?

Who we may see and who he may be
The question of whom, he does not speak?
He has some teeth, but has no beak
Some have seen him, but only a peek
Is he alive if he only walks the dead of night?

So, have you heard of The Owl Man?
WHO?
The Owl Man!
WHO?
Who is The Owl Man, to whom it may concern?

They say to him the word of man lost all meaning
So, what is the point in ever speaking
A hermit, a nomad what if he is no man?
A traveller, a vagabond
A simple searcher who looks from beyond

So, who is The Owl Man?
So, you really do not know?
No! Who is the who of who you speak?
Who is the Owl Man, to me it may concern?

He is a whom's who of who to whom it may concern.

Printed in Great Britain
by Amazon